THE BLACK SLEUTH

**Other titles in
The Northeastern Library of Black Literature
edited by Richard Yarborough**

THE BLACK SLEUTH

JOHN EDWARD BRUCE

Edited with an Introduction
by JOHN CULLEN GRUESSER

Northeastern University Press
BOSTON

Northeastern University Press

Library of Congress Cataloging-in-Publication Data
Bruce, John Edward.
 The Black sleuth / John Edward Bruce ; edited with an introduction
by John Cullen Gruesser.
  p. cm.—(The Northeastern library of Black literature)
 Includes bibliographical references.
 ISBN 1-55553-511-9 (acid-free paper)
  1. African American detectives—Fiction. 2. Americans—England—
Fiction. 3. England—Fiction. I. Gruesser, John Cullen, 1959– .
II. Title. III. Series.
PS3503.R876 B48 2002
813′.52—dc21   2001059188

Designed by Ann Twombly

Composed in Bodoni Book by The Composing Room of Michigan, Inc., Grand
Rapids, Michigan. Printed and bound by Maple Press, York, Pennsylvania. The
paper is Sebago Antique, an acid-free stock.

MANUFACTURED IN THE UNITED STATES OF AMERICA
06 05 04 03 02 5 4 3 2 1

In memory of
Mary Elizabeth Spilman Grosseholz
(1963–2001)

CONTENTS

INTRODUCTION

The Mysteries of *The Black Sleuth*

One of the earliest African American fictional works to depict a black detective and thus a forerunner of novels by writers such as Rudolph Fisher, Chester Himes, Walter Mosley, BarbaraNeely, and Valerie Wilson Wesley, John Edward Bruce's *The Black Sleuth* (1907– 09) is, in fact, only partially a mystery. The West African hero, Sadipe Okukenu, does not become a detective until the second half of the novel, and the crime he is investigating, the theft of a large, flawless diamond, never really takes place. Bruce's serial, however, is more than an idiosyncratic mystery story. Devoting nine of the novel's seventeen chapters to what will hereafter be called the African-abroad plot, Bruce uses a Black Atlantic perspective to evaluate white prejudice and racial injustice in the United States and elsewhere.[1] He does so not only to counter the anti-black propaganda and white man's burden rhetoric of the day but also to educate his African American readers about Africa, Western imperialism, and, perhaps most important, themselves. Moreover, through his protagonist's experiences in the American South, Bruce urges blacks to fight white racial intolerance and unleashes a potent attack on the accommodationist policies of the most influential turn-of-the-century African American leader, Booker T. Washington.

Bruce's serial and its attendant peculiarities raise a variety of baffling questions that will be addressed in the pages that follow. First, who was John E. Bruce and why is so little known about him today? Second, how does Bruce organize the story? Third, can a satisfactory resolution to the detective plot be pieced together from the often conflicting evidence provided? And, fourth, what is the publication history of this unique but obscure novel?

John Edward Bruce

Although John E. Bruce and Booker T. Washington differed greatly in ideological terms, these men led remarkably similar early lives.[2] Each was born a slave in 1856, Bruce in Maryland and Washington in Virginia. Largely self-taught, each started pursuing some form of higher education in 1872, Bruce studying at Howard University for three months and Washington enrolling at Hampton Institute, from which he graduated in 1875. Moreover, each became successful in his chosen profession at a young age. Beginning his career as a journalist in 1874, Bruce was writing for black and white newspapers by the age of twenty, started his own paper, the *Argus*, in 1879, and became a famous correspondent in the 1880s, adopting the pen name Bruce-Grit and contributing to more than one hundred black publications. I. Garland Penn in his late nineteenth-century survey of black newspapers and editors dubbed Bruce "the prince of Afro-American correspondents."[3] Washington, meanwhile, was appointed the first president of Tuskegee Institute at the age of twenty-five and oversaw its transformation from a makeshift school with only two buildings and a handful of students to a thriving institution with an extensive campus and a student body of more than a thousand. In 1896 he became the first African American to receive an honorary degree from Harvard, and the following year the president of the United States, William McKinley, commended him for what he had accomplished at Tuskegee. Bruce and Washington were also accomplished public speakers and advocates for black economic development and self-help. They split drastically, however, on the question of how to respond to white prejudice, discrimination, and violence.

In his famous 1895 Atlanta Exposition Address, Washington expresses his acceptance of segregation and asserts that "The wisest among my race understand that the agitation of questions of social equality is the extremist folly."[4] In contrast, Bruce consistently encouraged blacks in America and throughout the world to take action in defense of their rights. In an 1889 Washington, D.C., speech entitled "The Application of Force," Bruce not only states that "Agitation is a good thing; organization is a better thing" but admonishes blacks that they must be prepared to repay white violence in kind:

> Under the Mosaic dispensation, it was the custom to require "an eye for an eye and a tooth for a tooth." Under a no less Barbarous civilization than that which existed at that period of the world's history, let the Negro require at the hands of every white murderer in the South or elsewhere a life for a life. If they burn your houses, burn theirs. If they kill your wives and children, kill theirs. Pursue them relentlessly. Meet force with force, everywhere it is offered. If they demand blood, exchange with them until they are satiated. By a vigorous adherence to this course, the shedding of human blood by white men will soon become a thing of the past.[5]

A generation later, in a speech before the Sons of Africa, a society he organized in 1913, Bruce advocates a coordinated response to white tyranny, calling for cooperation among blacks in the United States, the West Indies, and Africa: "The psychological moment has I believe arrived for Negroes and colored men the world over to get together and fight for every right with all our might. We must organize to secure uniformity of utterance and action among the darker races and to meet organized wrong with intelligently organized resistance."[6]

Given the divergent political philosophies of the two men and Bruce's proclivity for speaking his mind, it should come as no surprise that the journalist was, as August Meier observes, "usually openly hostile to (and consistently suspected by)" the educator.[7] Like other opponents of Washington, Bruce stressed the need for higher education for African Americans, denouncing "the hog and hominy" policy of Tuskegee.[8] Moreover, he believed that the school's focus on vocational education had served only to heighten racial tension:

> Booker T. Washington's propaganda has not helped the Negro nearly as much as it has injured him. It has done this: it has called attention to Negro capacity for sustained effort along industrial lines, and this has exacted the jealousy . . . of a class of whites in this country which is more potent politically and numerically than the element which gives thousands for the upkeep of Tuskegee. This class of whites are they who are spreading the virus of race prejudice and the report that Negroes are being trained to take the places of white industrials.[9]

In a thoroughly condemnatory 1903 article, Bruce accuses Tuskegee of producing "*automatons*" and Washington of conspiring with the whites who support his school to discourage "any attempt to educate Negroes for the longer and more responsible duties of citizenship."[10] Describing Washington's edict that black Americans should avoid politics as "neither wise nor sincere," Bruce concludes by charging Tuskegee's president with being not only disingenuous and mercenary but also a traitor to his race:

> For a man who has never voted in his life, as he confesses, Mr. Washington's political activity and influence is greater than that of any veteran politician in the country. If the Negro can be kept in the background politically through Mr. Washington's influence for the next five years, he will become a complete political pariah. And that is the game now being played by Mr. Washington's rich white friends who have made him the star performer in the tragedy—the denouement of which is the undoing of the Negro by "the greatest Negro in

the world." The plot is as dazzling as it is spectacular and there's millions in it.[11]

In addition to his newspaper work and public addresses, Bruce wrote short books on African American history and political pamphlets, often publishing these at his own expense. He also belonged to several black organizations, including the American Negro Academy and the Negro Society for Historical Research (which he founded with Arthur Schomburg in 1911). He knew leading nineteenth-century figures such as Alexander Crummell and Edward Blyden, met and corresponded with Africans who had studied in or visited the United States, and contributed to African and West Indian periodicals as well as Duse Mohammed Ali's London-based *African Times and Orient Review*. As a result, he functioned as a conduit linking blacks of different generations and nationalities. In fact, Bruce served as one of Marcus Garvey's most important contacts when he arrived in America in 1916, writing letters of introduction for him to various race leaders. Although Bruce initially expressed skepticism about the Jamaican, he later changed his mind and in his final years devoted his talents and energy to implementing Garvey's program. He became a crucial liaison between the Universal Negro Improvement Association (UNIA) and African organizations, held the titles of Duke of the Nile and Duke of Uganda within the UNIA, wrote regularly for and helped to edit the UNIA's *Negro World,* and was accorded a hero's funeral at Liberty Hall in Harlem that was attended by more than five thousand people when he died in 1924.

How can Bruce be virtually unknown today when he attained such early and sustained journalistic success, wrote prolifically on a wide range of subjects and in various genres, and held key positions in several major African American and international black organizations? Noting that Bruce's audience was the black community exclusively, Peter Gilbert explains that he "evolved a determined militant stance that set him apart from the main streams of black thought as voiced by either Washington or W. E. B. Du Bois. He was one of the few black spokesman who saw no contradiction between emphasis on economic independence, self-help, race pride and race solidarity, and, on the other hand, emphasis on agitation for political and civil rights."[12] Building upon Gilbert, Ralph Crowder attributes Bruce's later obscurity to the fact that he, unlike Washington and Du Bois, was unwilling to court white recognition or approval: "He refused to join organizations supported or directed by whites. Thus, Bruce remained outside of 'white American History' and was excluded from its written registry."[13]

Bruce's name may also be unfamiliar because he failed to produce a major work elaborating his personal and political philosophy, along the lines of Washington's *Up from Slavery* (1901) and Du Bois's *The Souls of Black Folk* (1903). His only novel in book form, *The Awakening of Hezekiah Jones: A Story Dealing with Some of the Problems Affecting the Political Rewards Due the Negro* (1916), has received almost no critical attention. Likewise, although some of his newspaper pieces and speeches were published in 1971 in *The Selected Writings of John Edward Bruce,* the critical interest that this volume generated was quite limited and short-lived. Yet he deserves better, for, as Gilbert observes, "John Edward Bruce was a uniquely qualified and popular voice that spoke to and for America's black masses."[14] It is my hope that the publication of *The Black Sleuth* in the Northeastern Library of Black Literature series will inspire scholars, students, and other interested readers to learn more about Bruce, seek out additional works by him, and help restore this remarkable man to his rightful place in African American history and literature.

The Organization of The Black Sleuth

Readers of *The Black Sleuth* interested in solving the mystery will find themselves facing more of a challenge than they bargained for because the serial's detective plot is both problematic and unresolved. Before attempting to address this enigma, however, I want to demonstrate that Bruce's foremost concern is not the construction of a neatly organized story of ratiocination but rather white prejudice against blacks, particularly in the African-abroad plot that dominates chapters 2 through 10. In the very first sentence of the story, George De Forrest, an American sea captain residing in London, expresses his belief in black inferiority: "Do you mean to tell me that that nigger is a detective, and that you are going to put him on this case, Mr. Hunter?" (3). The novel shifts to Africa in chapters 2, 3, and 4, where we meet the protagonist Sadipe's brother, Mojola, whose physical, intellectual, and moral superiority over De Forrest powerfully refutes the American sailor's racist beliefs. Moreover, Mojola's experiences in England, which he recounts to the captain, suggest that white people's inflated opinion of themselves lacks justification. Following the fifth chapter, which indicts America's racial intolerance, chapters 6 through 10 concern Sadipe's sojourn in the United States, describing his studies in the North and his fiery baptism into Southern white prejudice, as well as black submission to it, both on his train trip south and during his short stay at an African American college. Appalled by what he beholds after crossing the Mason-Dixon line, Sadipe leaves the school, returns north, and takes a job with the International Detective Agency. Chapter 11 opens by informing readers that three years have passed, and then, finally, the detective plot begins in earnest. Even in the novel's last seven chapters, however, De Forrest's prejudiced doubts about Sadipe ring in the black sleuth's ears, spurring him on to capture the crooks and return the diamond to its owner.

In *The Black Sleuth*, Bruce did not write the first novel by a black American to depict either Africa or Africans; however, he was the first with extensive knowledge of contemporary Africa to do so. Martin Delany's *Blake; or, The Huts of America* (1859–60) contains a brief and not particularly memorable description of the continent, and Sutton Griggs's *Unfettered* (1902) depicts what may be the first African character of any significance in African American fiction in a fascinating chapter entitled "A Street Parade."[15] Griggs also sets a portion of his next novel, *The Hindered Hand* (1905),[16] in Liberia, yet these works indicate that he knew little about the continent and held inconsistent views about Africans. In contrast, Pauline Hopkins, whose 1902–03 serial *Of One Blood; or, the Hidden Self* portrays an ancient and still-functioning Ethiopian kingdom in what today is northern Sudan, possessed considerable knowledge about the continent's past, some of which she incorporates into her story in an attempt to educate her *Colored American Magazine* readers.[17] Like Bruce, whose serial is much more than a typical detective story, Hopkins constructs her novel as a literary hybrid, grafting several different genres onto the African adventure tale. Although she, too, predicts a bright future for the continent, Hopkins, unlike Bruce, displays ambivalence about contemporary Africa and Western imperialism.

In the African-abroad plot of *The Black Sleuth,* Bruce both dislocates white American characters in order to hold their prejudiced beliefs and language up to scrutiny and enables his readers to see England and the United States through African eyes. Bruce takes De Forrest first to London, where this son of a slave ship captain is portrayed as being at odds with his environment: "Although he was an American by birth, he was English by adoption, but with the foolish American antipathy and prejudice to people of darker hue" (5). In the second chapter, this dislocation intensifies when Bruce shifts the setting to South Africa. Here, much to his chagrin, De Forrest finds himself being lectured about Africa's past and future greatness and the Western world's greed by a black man who is better educated and more eloquent than he. In chapter 5, Bruce again displaces a white American character, this time transporting a Northern ship captain to Yorubaland, where the seaman encourages Sadipe's father to allow his son to travel to the United States. Unlike De Forrest, the "downeaster" Captain Barnard, "like most of the men from that part of America, . . . had a great deal of sympathy for the Negro" (22). Nevertheless, the rhetoric he uses differs only slightly from that of his blatantly racist compatriot; for example, Barnard asserts that a sojourn in the United States would enable Sadipe to contribute to "the uplift of his 'benighted race'" (22). Furthermore, the Northerner states that "America is the most Christian country on the globe" and contends that the elder Okukenu "could not send Sadipe to a better place than America; it is a progressive country, and black men there enjoy the same rights as white men" (23). However, the captain soon finds himself called upon to answer for the racial injustice in his homeland when Sadipe's father asks him about the United States' past history of slavery and present practice of lynching. In part because of the honesty of the American's answer to this question, which "made him blush for shame for the 'most Christian nation on earth'" (24), Sadipe is allowed to accompany Barnard.

When *The Black Sleuth* shifts to America in chapters 6 through 10, Bruce enables his readers to observe race relations in the United States from an African point of view. After a benign eighteen months spent in Maine under the tutelage of Barnard's sister, Sadipe travels south to attend the fictitious Eckington College for Colored Youth. Insulted by a ticket-taker at the train station in Washington, D.C., and later threatened with physical violence for his defiant refusal to move to the Jim Crow car, Sadipe is further dismayed when he sees the conditions at the Negro college. In a thinly veiled attack on Washington and the Tuskegee Institute, Bruce depicts the open hostility of the whites in the town to the school, the low academic standards of the college, and the cowardice and hypocrisy of its principal, Professor Swift (whose name may be intended to lampoon Washington's nickname, "the Wizard"). When Sadipe learns from Swift of the rigidly enforced segregation within the town, he declares, "This is all very strange, indeed. I had no idea that human beings could be so intolerant of the rights of others, and all this in free America! I cannot understand it, sir" (39). Swift's pathetic response contrasts sharply with the boldness Sadipe exhibited on the train: "Neither can we . . . but we are obliged to submit to these things because we are helpless, and can do no better" (39). Through his depiction of the school, the surrounding community, and Swift's accommodationism, Bruce throws an ironic light upon the principal's fund-raising trips in which he tells "northern audiences what a wonderful work he was doing down South toward the moral redemption and regeneration of the colored race, and how badly he needed an endowment of $30,000 to put it on its feet, so that it could begin the work of solving on practical lines the race problem which is still with us" (39). *The Black Sleuth* thus serves as an important precursor to Ralph Ellison's *Invisible Man* (1952), which features an unflattering portrait of a Tuskegee-like college headed by the duplicitous Dr. Bledsoe.

Before Sadipe begins his detective career, Bruce extends the African-abroad plot to give the lie once more to anti-black propaganda and white man's burden rhetoric as well as their internalization by some black Americans. On the day that Sadipe leaves the college, he and the other students attend a talk by Rev. Silas Skinner, a white Southerner who has served as a missionary in Africa. After the speech, Swift praises Skinner's zeal and "self-sacrificing spirit" in carrying "the message of good-will and brotherhood to those who sit in darkness" (47–48) and then calls upon Sadipe to make a comment. As in the exchange between De Forrest and Mojola, Sadipe's oratorical prowess and superior knowledge contrast with Skinner's platitudes and misinformation. The Yoruba points out that "the so-called 'heathens' of Africa are not nearly so barbarous and inhospitable to the stranger within their gates, nor are they as inhuman and bloodthirsty as the so-called civilized white Christians of the South, who burn Negroes at the stake and hang them from trees and telegraph poles, as I have learned that they do, since my sojourn in this country" (48). Echoing sentiments expressed by Bruce in speeches and pamphlets, such as "The Blot on the Escutcheon" (1890) and "The Blood Red Record" (1901),[18] Sadipe's assertion bears a striking resemblance to a declaration made by Prince Momolu Massaquoi, the son of Sierra Leonean royalty and a student at Nashville's Central Tennessee College, when he addressed a meeting of American clergymen in 1894. Despite Americans' talk about the "savage in Africa," Massaquoi, who witnessed a lynching in Nashville in 1892, contended that in the United States there was "more savagery than I have seen in all my days in Africa."[19] In Sadipe's rebuttal, which nearly results in a white race riot, he goes on to make a prediction that recalls both his brother's statements to De Forrest and Bruce's own ideas about the future: "The [characteristics of the] so-called weaker races, whose weakness consists in being unlike the Anglo in that they do not covet their neighbors' goods and are not engaged in cruel warfare to extend their power, . . . will prove the sources of their greatest strength when the awakening of nations, which is fast approaching, takes place" (49). Significantly, the African's statements succeed in converting his fellow students—as they presumably converted many of Bruce's black readers—to a new way of looking at Africa and themselves.

The African-abroad plot and the detective plot of *The Black Sleuth* are not, in fact, as discrete as they first appear. In the early chapters of the novel, Bruce implies that the father of Mojola and Sadipe Okukenu agrees to allow his sons to journey abroad for politically strategic reasons and not because he wants them to be "civilized" and "Christianized." The Yoruba knows his sons will not be happy in the West, but he sends them on what amount to spy missions to "learn more about the white man in his native land" (10). Looking at Sadipe's student years in the United States in this light, it becomes clear that the African-abroad plot makes the detective plot possible. On the one hand, Sadipe's American experiences provide the future detective with important insight into the (white) criminal mind. His encounters with rude, conceited, prejudiced, and acquisitive white Southerners prove invaluable, enabling him to thwart the schemes of the confidence men he later pursues, such as Bradshawe and his gang. On the other hand, Bruce suggests that all of the time Sadipe has spent in the West, first as a student in the United States and later as a detective in England and on the European mainland, will help him protect his people from the designs of colonialists and imperialists when he returns to Africa. Moreover, Sadipe's skills as a crime solver offer yet another refutation of white assumptions of black inferiority. As Stephen Soitos observes, the "choice of a detective format for African intellectual revisionism makes absolute sense considering the classical model of ratiocination developed by Poe. . . . Bruce's master stroke was in taking popular culture's most accepted model of intellectual superiority—the detective—and turning him into a black African who is more rational than and hence superior to any white in the book."[20]

In addition to implicitly designating his protagonist's past experiences as a factor contributing to his success as a sleuth, Bruce also explicitly credits Sadipe's heritage for his superior memory for faces and his uncanny powers of detection. Like the early Du Bois, Bruce believed that each race had inherited talents for certain arts, sciences, and endeavors that distinguished it from other peoples. Scholars have termed this view "racialism," which Kwame Anthony Appiah defines as the belief "that there are heritable characteristics, possessed by members of our species, which allow us to divide them into a small set of races, in such a way that all members of these races share certain traits and tendencies with each other that they do not share with members of any other race."[21] Sadipe needs to look carefully at a person only once and he is able to recall his or her features forever. The Yoruba specifically connects this gift to his origins, informing his boss, Mr. Hunter, that "an African, and I am told that a North American Indian, never forget a face they have once seen" (74). He also has such highly developed powers of observation that he apparently sniffs out the criminal conspiracy of Bradshawe and his cohorts before they have a chance to concoct it. Unlike De Forrest, the jewelers Cheltenham and Sykes, and even Hunter himself, who met Bradshawe a few years earlier, Sadipe suspects that the "colonel" is a fraud from the very beginning and quickly proves this. Similarly, in the novel's final chapters, he tells the fortunes of the adventuress Miss Crenshawe and her servants with astounding accuracy. When his boss praises his soothsaying skills, he denies that some occult knowledge was responsible for his success and hints that he relied instead on Sherlock Holmes–like deduction: "Sadipe laughed heartily at the compliment, and said that he did not know one card from another, and that he had merely guessed at the things he told the girls which had pleased them so much and their mistress, to whom his message had given such evident pain" (92).

Bruce makes clear that it is the combination of Sadipe's innate abilities and his dark complexion that proves to be his greatest weapon as a sleuth. Exploiting the low opinion most whites have of blacks, he uses his status as an Ellisonian invisible man to his advantage. In a passage that echoes Bruce's own racialist beliefs, Hunter tells his ace detective, "You Africans have many advantages over us Europeans, and there are some things which you can do better than we when you try. Your black face will be an important aid in the capture of [Bradshawe] (if you capture him), and your knowledge of French will come in handy, for in the presence of strangers he always converses in that language, and he will never suspect that you understand that tongue" (76). Moreover, as Soitos notes, "Because of his outsider status in white society he is acutely aware of masks and masking, as well as being capable, in the trickster tradition, of assuming disguises to outwit his opponents."[22] Sadipe, in fact, convincingly impersonates a waiter, an African student, a peddler, and a rich African merchant in his pursuit of the would-be diamond thieves, who are themselves experts at disguise.

The fact that the African detective's skin color "disarm[s] all suspicion as to his true character" (67), however, only serves to underscore the persistent fact of white racism. In this sense, Bruce's story closely resembles Pauline Hopkins's serial *Hagar's Daughter: A Story of Southern Caste Prejudice* (1901–02), the earliest-known African American novel to feature a black detective.[23] Like Sadipe, Hopkins's sleuth, the young maid Venus Johnson, succeeds in putting a stop to the criminal conspiracy in the story; however, *Hagar's Daughter* ends on a somber note because the greater crime of white racial intolerance continues unabated. Likewise, Bruce's novel ultimately suggests that even the most talented black sleuth, on his own or with the aid of enlightened whites like Hunter and General De Mortie (who comes to Sadipe's assistance on the train and helps him secure his job as a detective), cannot break up the greatest conspiracy of all—that of prejudice against people of color in the United States and abroad. Instead, its defeat can apparently be attained only through black solidarity and coordinated resistance.

The Detective Plot of The Black Sleuth

The question of whether it is possible to make sense of the detective plot of *The Black Sleuth* still remains. The challenge is formidable not only because Bruce certainly seems to have been more attentive to the African-abroad plot than to the detective plot but also because the serial is riddled with contradictions and often eschews chronological order. The opening chapter of Bruce's story informs readers that an American sea captain residing in London engages the International Detective Agency to solve a case involving "the loss of an uncut diamond, which had been stolen" (4); however, although subsequent chapters refer to this theft, the crime has not yet occurred at the conclusion of the novel. Moreover, although the beginning of chapter 11 refers to Sadipe's career as "an Iliad of successes" culminating in "the hour he rounded up on foreign shore four of the most skillful swindlers on the continent of Europe" (57), the novel stops before this capture takes place. Even more perplexing—or perhaps the most convincing proof of the protagonist's superior skills as a detective—is the fact that Sadipe puts the suspected perpetrators under surveillance *before* they steal the diamond, disguising himself as a waiter to eavesdrop on their plans to filch the gem. Further complicating matters, the events in most of chapter 13, all of chapter 14, and the opening paragraph of chapter 15 occur prior to those recounted in the second half of chapter 12. What follows is my attempt to break down the novel into its basic plot elements to produce a time line that includes (A) an event recounted in the story that takes place before the earliest scenes depicted in the serial, (B) events that occur or are referred to during the story proper, and (C) events that occur (or are likely to occur) after the serial comes to an end, including one that is described in the serial's opening chapter and another that is alluded to in chapter 11. I have indicated parenthetically in which chapters specific events are depicted or referred to.

The Plot Elements of The Black Sleuth

A
Majola journeys to England, returning to Africa after a brief sojourn there. (2 and 3)

B
Barnard asks Sadipe's father for permission to take Sadipe to America. (5)

Sadipe journeys to Maine and studies there for eighteen months. (6)

Hunter founds the International Detective Agency. (6)

Sadipe travels south by train and stays briefly at Eckington College. (6–10)

Sadipe journeys north to join the International Detective Agency. (10)

Sadipe enjoys great success as a detective. (Mentioned in 11)

Hunter unwittingly encounters Bradshawe in Vienna in 1899. (Mentioned in 14)

Mojola, now a teacher, meets De Forrest in Kimberley and sells him the diamond. (2–4)

De Forrest returns to London and takes the diamond to the jewelers. (11)

Bradshawe learns about the diamond. (12)

Sadipe encounters Bradshawe in Mr. Stoughton's room at the Royal Arms Hotel. (13)

Sadipe informs Hunter about this encounter and puts Bradshawe under surveillance. (13 and 14)

Sadipe sees Bradshawe at a music hall and follows him home. (14)

Sadipe tails Bradshawe and Miss Crenshawe to the Royal Arms. (14)

Sadipe informs Hunter of Bradshawe's whereabouts. (14)

Sadipe secures a job as a waiter at the Royal Arms. (12)

Crenshawe has lunch at the Royal Arms and attracts De Forrest's attention. (12)

Bradshawe meets De Forrest in the smoking room of the Royal Arms. (15)

Bradshawe throws a party for De Forrest, where the captain meets Crenshawe. (15)

Bradshawe and his gang meet at the Royal Arms to plan the diamond heist and their escape. (15)

De Forrest goes to the house where Crenshawe lives. (Mentioned in 17)

De Forrest leaves for the East Indies. (Mentioned in 16)

Sadipe goes to the conspirators' house disguised as a peddler selling curios. (15)

Sadipe tells the fortunes of two female servants and Crenshawe. (15 and 16)

Sadipe reports his progress to Hunter and sees a newspaper article about the conspirators. (17)

Sadipe returns to the house to tell fortunes and learns the conspirators are in Rouen. (17)

C

Crenshawe steals the diamond at the second party for De Forrest, which she hosts. (?)

The conspirators escape to Paris and then Belgium. (?)

De Forrest enlists Hunter's detective agency to recover the diamond and insults Sadipe. (1)

Sadipe captures the conspirators in Europe. (Mentioned in 11)

Sadipe recovers the diamond when he apprehends the thieves.
(?)
De Forrest is forced to repudiate his earlier doubts about Sadipe.
(?)
Sadipe decides to return to Africa. (?)

As this list indicates, much of what will transpire after the events narrated in the story can be pieced together from the information the serial provides, in spite of its many inconsistencies. Presumably, De Forrest returns from his voyage, retrieves the cut and polished diamond from the jewelers (even though chapter 1 states that the pilfered gem is "uncut"), and has it stolen from him by Miss Crenshawe at the second party given in his honor by Bradshawe and his cohorts, who then drug him and deposit him in a disreputable location, as they plotted to do at the lunch at the Royal Arms described in chapter 15. Very likely it is upon recovering his wits that De Forrest seeks the help of Mr. Hunter and expresses his prejudiced skepticism about Sadipe's abilities, which is the episode that starts the serial. After the thieves obtain the diamond, it follows that they flee to Paris and quickly move on to Belgium, intending to take a steamer to the United States, in keeping with the plan overheard by Sadipe; however, the black sleuth follows them to the European mainland, where he succeeds in capturing them, as the reader learns in chapter 11, and recovering the diamond.

Although the above scenario resolves the detective plot, two other developments would help to bring the African-abroad plot and thus *The Black Sleuth* as a whole to closure. First, because of the repeated references in the serial to the racist doubts about Sadipe's abilities expressed by De Forrest at the opening of the story, it would be appropriate for the captain to take back his words and acknowledge the African's talents when confronted with the evidence of Sadipe's success in solving the case. Second, given the serial's prolonged attention to Sadipe's father and brother, its denunciation of white Western materialism and imperialism, and its emphasis on Africa's future, it would also be fitting if Sadipe, after solving the case and receiving an apology from De Forrest, were to announce his determination to return to his homeland.

The Publication History of The Black Sleuth

Dating *The Black Sleuth* presents serious challenges. The only known extant copy is in the John Edward Bruce Papers at the New York Public Library's Schomburg Center for Research in Black Culture.[24] The manuscript itself is not available to the public; however, the serial, along with the rest of the voluminous Bruce Papers, can be accessed on microfilm.[25] The novel was printed in *McGirt's Magazine*, a successful early black publication based in Philadelphia whose highest estimated circulation, according to Walter Daniel, was 1500.[26] Penelope Bullock reports that publication of *McGirt's* began in 1903 (probably in August) and that the magazine ran monthly until August 1908. A new series began in 1909, when the journal came out on a quarterly basis, and then it ceased publication.[27] Determining precisely in which issues of the journal *The Black Sleuth* appeared is difficult for two reasons. First, according to Bullock, only seventeen of the fifty or more issues of *McGirt's* that were published survive, and these are scattered among various libraries.[28] Second, in only a few instances do the pages of the novel from *McGirt's* in the Bruce Papers indicate the issues in which specific installments were published. *The Black Sleuth* runs seventeen chapters and appeared in seventeen installments, but these are not identical—the first installment contains chapters one and two, and the last chapter is split between the final two installments. Several corrections and some marginal notes, presumably by Bruce, appear on the pages from *McGirt's* in the Bruce Papers, including chapter numbers in many cases. At the top of the tenth installment, the words "Chap 11" and what seems to be "May" (most likely referring to the May 1908 issue of *McGirt's)* have been written in by hand. Notes that read "Jun" and "Chap 12" on the page preceding the start of the next installment indicate that chapter 12 appeared in the June 1908 issue of the journal. Written at the top of the first page of the twelfth installment is the number "13" and the word "July" in pen and "August" in pencil; as the pencil corrections seem to have been added after those in ink, the latter date is likely the correct one. Penned on the first page of the thirteenth installment are the words "Sept 1908" and "Chap XIV." The fifteenth installment has the notes "XVI" (apparently the chapter number) and what appears to be "Janu Feb Mar" (probably referring to the January/February/March 1909 issue of *McGirt's*) written at the top of the first page. Although the shorter section of chapter 17 comes before the longer one in the Bruce Papers (and this is the way the serial appears in the microfilm version of the Bruce Papers), it is likely that these final two installments were either inadvertently shuffled—perhaps even by Bruce himself; the pages are unbound—or deliberately reordered by someone at the Schomburg Center who noticed that the shorter section ends with the words "(*To be continued.*),*" while the longer one does not. However, the handwritten note "April 1909," no doubt referring to the April/May/June issue of *McGirt's*, on the page (19) that precedes the longer section of chapter 17, which runs from pages 20 to 23, indicates that it should come before the shorter section of this chapter, which must have appeared in the next issue of the journal. Working from these clues (and assuming that the serial appeared in every issue of *McGirt's* that was published during the time that it ran), I estimate that *The Black Sleuth* began in August 1907 and ended with the July/August/September 1909 issue.[29] According to the data supplied by Bullock, twelve issues of *McGirt's* appeared in 1907 and seven in 1908, January through June and an August issue.[30] If my dating of the serial is correct, there must have been two additional issues of *McGirt's* in 1908 that Bullock does not list—one in September and one in October, November, or December or an October/November/December issue. The table below lists the corresponding date, issue number, chapters, and page numbers for each of the seventeen installments of the serial.

The Black Sleuth in McGirt's Magazine

In yet another mystery relating to *The Black Sleuth*, the Bruce Papers contain a partial, alternative version of the serial. At least the first four chapters of the story, which resemble but are by no means identical with those that appeared in *McGirt's Magazine*, were published in a newspaper apparently entitled the *Progressive American* (the first word is unclear). Bruce pasted these chapters into the opening pages of a now rapidly disintegrating political handbook, along with what seems to be the paper's masthead listing John L. Waller and Clifton G. A. French as "Editors and Proprietors" and "28 W. 134 St. New York City" as the address. These undated columns of crumbling and nearly brown newsprint have some notes in pen and pencil (including one that says "McGirt") written on them. In addition, on a small piece of paper there is a handwritten note, presumably by Bruce, reading, "V VI VII VIII IX X XI XII XIII XIV XV—Missing Chapters to be clipped and pasted," suggesting that the alternative version ran for a considerable period in the newspaper but Bruce never got around to gluing the rest of it into the political handbook. James Danky reports that John L.Waller edited the *American Citizen* of Kansas City in 1896 and 1897;[31] however, I have been unable to locate any references to or information about his and French's *Progressive American.* Interestingly, Gilbert states that early in his journalistic career, in the mid-1870s, Bruce "became the special correspondent of *The Progressive American,* published by John Freeman, a pioneer journalist."[32] At this point, it is impossible to state definitively whether this other version of *The Black Sleuth* was published before, after, or around the same time as the one that appeared in *McGirt's Magazine.* However, because of Mojola's reference to the death of Cecil Rhodes in chapter 4, the alternative version could have been published no earlier than 1902.

Editor's Note

In transcribing *The Black Sleuth* from the pages of *McGirt's Magazine* in the Bruce Papers, I have striven for fidelity, consistency, clarity, and readability. All of the italicized words and all of the parentheses (including those surrounding question marks) in the present text are found in the Bruce Papers. Moreover, all of the legible handwritten emendations, presumably made by Bruce himself, have been incorporated into the text. I have corrected, without notation, most of the grammatical and typographic errors and regularized punctuation and spelling. In those cases where the text makes no sense or something is clearly missing, I have added words or punctuation in square brackets for the sake of comprehensibility or pointed out the problem in an endnote. Certain errors and handwritten corrections that appear frequently have been annotated. In addition, I have deleted the first eleven paragraphs of chapter 7 from the main text because they repeat, often in the same words, the final seven paragraphs of chapter 6. Appendix A presents the opening of the seventh chapter exactly as it appears in the Bruce Papers.

My most significant change has been to reverse the order of the final two installments of the serial as they appear in the microfilm version of the Bruce Papers. In addition to the note "April 1909" that precedes the longer section of the final chapter, which I have discussed above, the internal evidence strongly suggests that the two parts of chapter 17 somehow became inverted. The sequence of the penultimate and final sections on microfilm is problematic for three reasons. First, one of the shortest installments of the entire novella, the part of chapter 17 that is presented first in the microfilm version and last here begins abruptly, with Sadipe back at Bradshawe's house without any explanation. Second, everything that Sadipe learns from the maid in this installment and the secret he imparts to her seem to be totally disregarded in the longer section of chapter 17. Wouldn't the detective report to his boss immediately after his first visit to the house rather than the second, and why would he expect the maid to still be there after he has advised her to get away as soon as possible? Third, the reference to the "Count" by Sadipe is odd. Up until this point, there has been no mention of a count—other than Bradshawe himself in disguise—being connected with the thieves. (Throughout the serial, in fact, it is never clear exactly who the "quartet" of conspirators is. Is it Bradshawe, Crenshawe, Hodder, and Hodder's lady friend or, as the final two installments suggest, Bradshawe, Crenshawe, Hodder, and the unnamed count?) When the order of the two parts of chapter 17 is reversed, however, the serial flows more smoothly and makes much more sense. Sadipe reports directly to Hunter after his first visit to Bradshawe's house; at the manager's office, he gets the clue from the *Times* that Bradshawe, Hodder, and the "Count" are in Rouen; he then returns to the house the next day under the pretense of telling fortunes, learns more about the thieves' whereabouts (including confirmation that the conspirators are in Rouen), and urges the maid to leave the house as rapidly as she can. Appendix B preserves the order of the concluding chapter as it appears on microfilm.

JOHN CULLEN GRUESSER

Introduction

Notes

Some of the material in this Introduction and in the endnotes to the text has appeared in different form in my book *Black on Black: Twentieth-Century African American Literature about Africa* (Lexington: University Press of Kentucky, 2000).

1. See Paul Gilroy, *The Black Atlantic: Modernity and Double Consciousness* (Cambridge: Harvard University Press, 1993), in which the author regards the Atlantic as a "single, complex unit of analysis" connecting black people in Africa, Europe, and the Americas (15).

2. For information on Bruce's life and career, see Penelope Bullock, *The Afro-American Periodical Press, 1838–1909* (Baton Rouge: Louisiana State University Press, 1981), 78; Ralph Crowder, "John Edward Bruce: Pioneer Black Nationalist," *Afro-Americans in New York Life and History* 2.2 (July 1978): 47–66, "Street Scholars: Self-Trained Black Historians," *Black Collegian* 9.3 (January–February, 1979): 8, 10, 12, 14, 16, 18, 20, 22, and 80, and "John Edward Bruce, Edward Wilmot Blyden, Alexander Crummell, and J. Robert Love: Mentors, Patrons, and the Evolution of a Pan-African Intellectual Network," *Afro-Americans in New York Life and History* 20.2 (July 1996): 59–91; William H. Ferris, *The African Abroad, or His Evolution in Western Civilization* (1913; reprint, New York: Johnson, 1968), 2: 80–86; Milfred C. Fierce, *The Pan-African Idea in the United States 1900–1919* (New York: Garland, 1993), 50–54; Peter Gilbert, "The Life and Thought of John Edward Bruce," in *The Selected Writings of John Edward Bruce: Militant Black Journalist,* ed. Peter Gilbert (New York: Arno, 1971), 1–9; John Gruesser, "Bruce, John E.," in *Oxford Companion to African American Literature,* ed. William L. Andrews, Trudier Harris, and Frances Smith Foster (New York: Oxford University Press, 1997), 108; "John Edward Bruce: Three Documents," in *Dictionary of Literary Biography,* vol. 50, *Afro-American Writers before the Harlem Renaissance,* ed. Trudier Harris and Thadious M. Davis (Detroit: Gale Research, 1986), 298–305; Ernest Kaiser, "Bruce, John Edward," in *Dictionary of Negro Biography,* ed. Rayford W. Logan and Michael R. Winston (New York: Norton, 1989), 76–77; Tony Martin, *Race First: The Ideological and Organizational Struggles of Marcus Garvey and the Universal Negro Improvement Association* (Westport, Conn.: Greenwood,

1976), esp. 36 and 82–83; August Meier, *Negro Thought in America, 1880–1915*, 2d ed. (Ann Arbor: University of Michigan Press, 1988), 262–63; and Lawrence D. Reddick, "Biographical Sketch of John Edward Bruce," John Edward Bruce Collection, Schomburg Center for Research in Black Culture, New York Public Library, New York. For *The Black Sleuth*'s connection to other works of African American detective fiction, see Stephen F. Soitos, *The Blues Detective: A Study of African American Detective Fiction* (Amherst: University of Massachusetts Press, 1996); Paula L. Woods, Introduction to *Spooks, Spies, and Private Eyes: Black Mystery, Crime, and Suspense Fiction*, ed. Paula L. Woods (New York: Doubleday, 1995), xii–xviii; and Gary Phillips, "The Cool, the Square and the Tough: The Archetypes of Black Male Characters in Mystery and Crime Fiction," *Black Scholar* 28.1 (Spring 1998): 27–32.

3. I. Garland Penn, *The Afro-American Press and Its Editors* (1891; reprint, New York: Arno, 1969), 346.

4. Booker T. Washington, *Up from Slavery* (1901; reprint, New York: Signet, 2000), 155.

5. John E. Bruce, "The Application of Force" (1889), in Gilbert, *Selected Writings of Bruce*, 32.

6. Bruce, "Sons of Africa" (1913), in *Apropos of Africa: Sentiments of Negro American Leaders on Africa from the 1800s to the 1950s*, ed. Adelaide Cromwell Hill and Martin Kilson (London: Cass, 1969), 173–74.

7. Meier, *Negro Thought in America*, 263.

8. Bruce quoted in Reddick, "Biographical Sketch," 2.

9. Bruce, "White Opposition to the Negro" (1900?), in Gilbert, *Selected Writings of Bruce*, 62.

10. Bruce, "Industrial Education" (1903), in Gilbert, *Selected Writings of Bruce*, 88.

11. Ibid.

12. Gilbert, *Selected Writings of Bruce*, 4.

13. Crowder, "John Edward Bruce," 62.

14. Gilbert, *Selected Writings of Bruce*, 9.

15. Martin Delany, *Blake; or, The Huts of America*, ed. Floyd J. Miller (1859–60; reprint, Boston: Beacon, 1970); Sutton E. Griggs, *Unfettered. A Novel* (1902; reprint, New York: AMS, 1971).

16. Sutton E. Griggs, *The Hindered Hand; or, The Reign of the Repressionist*, 3d ed. (1905; reprint, New York: AMS, 1969).

17. Pauline E. Hopkins, *Of One Blood; Or, the Hidden Self*, in *The Magazine Novels of Pauline Hopkins* (New York: Oxford University Press, 1988), 439–621.

18. Bruce, "The Blot on the Escutcheon," in Gilbert, *Selected Writings of Bruce*, 33–43, and "The Blood Red Record," ibid., 68–84.

19. Massaquoi is quoted in Michael McCarthy, *Dark Continent: Africa as Seen by Americans* (Westport, Conn.: Greenwood, 1983), 148.

20. Soitos, *Blues Detective*, 78.

21. Kwame Anthony Appiah, *In My Father's House: Africa in the Philosophy of Culture* (New York: Oxford University Press, 1992), 13.

22. Soitos, *Blues Detective*, 87.

23. Hopkins, *Hagar's Daughter: A Story of Southern Caste Prejudice*, in *The Magazine Novels of Pauline Hopkins* (New York: Oxford University Press, 1988), 1–284.

24. Bruce, *The Black Sleuth*, John Edward Bruce Collection, Box 6, Schomburg Center for Research in Black Culture.

25. Ibid., Microfilm Reel 3.

26. Walter C. Daniel, *Black Journals of the United States* (Westport, Conn.: Greenwood, 1982), 241.

27. Bullock, *Afro-American Periodical Press*, 252.

28. Ibid.

29. Librarians at Atlanta University, which has the only surviving copy of the October/November/December 1909 issue of *McGirt's*, informed me via telephone that the magazine's swan song does not contain an installment of *The Black Sleuth*.

30. Bullock, *Afro-American Periodical Press*, 253.

31. James Danky, *African American Newspapers and Periodicals: A National Bibliography* (Cambridge: Harvard University Press, 1998), 40.

32. Gilbert, *Selected Writings of Bruce*, 4.

Written Expressly for *McGirt's Magazine*

THE BLACK SLEUTH

An Original Story
By J. E. Bruce-Grit[1]

CHAPTER I

"Do you mean to tell me that that nigger is a detective, and that you are going to put him on this case, Mr. Hunter?"

The speaker was Capt. George De Forrest, a somewhat choleric and impulsive person, who would easily be mistaken for a gentleman—only gentlemen do not use the word "nigger" when speaking of Negroes, nor spell it with two gs when writing about them.

The question was addressed to Mr. Samuel Hunter (very appropriately named), who was the manager of the International Detective Agency, a private concern which had achieved considerable success in the apprehension and conviction of at least a dozen famous burglars, notably the daring safe-cracker O'Brien, who got away with $400,000 in cash and bonds a few years ago, in Chicago, and Keene, the great counterfeiter, who for five years had successfully defied detection and baffled and thwarted the best men in the U.S. Secret Service.

The running down of these notoriously clever criminals gave the International Detective Agency high standing, and resulted in increasing its yearly revenues a hundred fold.

It had branch offices in all the great capitals of Europe, and it employed hundreds of trained thief catchers—men of every civilized race, who thoroughly understood their business, and generally got whatever they went after.

3

The conversation above recorded took place in the London office of the agency, and related to the loss of an uncut diamond, which had been stolen from Captain De Forrest, an American seafaring man engaged in the East India trade. Mr. Hunter, having gotten the details of the Captain's story and a retainer, announced his purpose to assign an intelligent young African in the employ of the agency—a Yoruba[2] man—to the case, knowing that if the facts stated by the Captain were what he said they were, the Negro would run down the thief, or thieves.

But the Captain's American prejudice got the better of his judgment and good taste, and impelled him to make the coarse and insulting remarks quoted.

The "Nigger," whose black face had been the cause of the remark, was from the Ekiti County[3] in Yorubaland on the West Coast, and was one of the most valuable men in the service of the agency. He was well educated, having graduated from Eton College, in England, with high honors,[4] a fine linguist, an expert at chess, and as perfectly developed physically as an Apollo Belvidere.[5] Yet, with all of his natural and acquired attainments, he was the personification of modesty and good breeding.

The gruff old sea dog had not meant that his words should be heard by the "nigger"; yet, nevertheless, they were heard, and the "nigger" then and there registered a vow that he would make that particular captain own the force of his genius and feel very much ashamed of himself by showing him how cleverly a "nigger" can do his work.

Captain De Forrest was of Southern birth. His father, Gamaliel De Forrest, a Louisianian, had been captain of a slaver, and when Congress, in 1808, forbade the further importation of African slaves into the United States by law, he went to the East Indies with his young wife and son,[6] and took service on one of the vessels of the East India Company[7] as captain.

The boy followed the sea from his tenth year, and from his father, who was an experienced navigator, he acquired a practical knowledge of navigation.

On his twenty-eighth birthday, through the influence of his father, he was made captain of the "Norman K. Peters," a merchant vessel trading in the East Indies and other ports, and for forty years he ploughed the raging main from the Occident to the Orient, visiting nearly every country on the globe.

In each port that he visited he procured some valuable memento of his visit to adorn his personal residence in the suburbs of London. Although he was an American by birth, he was English by adoption, but with the foolish American antipathy and prejudice to people of darker hue.

As already stated, nearly every country on the globe had been laid under tribute to him or his agents, so that he possessed a collection of rare curios and bric-a-brac of almost priceless value.

There were jade vases from China, handsomely wrought rugs from Persia, coats of armor from Japan, swords of curious design from Damascus, pipes of intrinsic value from the Ottoman Empire, articles fashioned from ebony, mahogany and gold from the Dark Continent, precious stones, pins, rings, watches and an endless variety of things from almost every country where such things are used.

CHAPTER II

In South Africa, whither he had journeyed to take on a cargo of hides and other native products, Captain De Forrest had had the good fortune to meet at Kimberley, where the famous diamond mines are located (which made Cecil Rhodes, as they are making hundreds of others, rich beyond the dreams of avarice, yet are still avaricious), a young African of possibly nineteen or twenty, who was wandering aimlessly, as it seemed to him, in the direction of his vessel, along the water front.[8]

He was a magnificent type of African young manhood, tall—fully six feet—and physically well developed. He was attired in the full dress usually affected by the African on his native heath—a loin cloth of white material—and wore on his head a delicately wrought cap without a visor made of the native grass of the country. As he strolled leisurely along the water front he seemed to enjoy the cool and refreshing breezes wafted shoreward by the trade winds from the broad expanse of old ocean, and to be at peace with all the world.

There was something in his bearing that attracted the captain's attention. He held his head high and walked with the precision of one who had seen service as a soldier. As he came nearer to where Captain De Forrest and a group of British officers were standing, chatting of one thing and another, the captain, espying him, exclaimed, "Gad, gentlemen, there is the finest looking black fellow I ever saw," pointing towards the approaching figure, who was all unconscious of the fact that he was an object of admiration, and that, too, by an American with no particular fancy for Negroes. "Look!" said the captain to his friends. "He is as straight as an arrow; what muscles, what a chest development, what a splendid bearing. Gad! He is a picture."

The Englishmen, who had many times seen the African at his best, and even more perfect types than the young man in question, did not enthuse over him as much as did Captain De Forrest, though they very frankly admitted that he was not bad to look upon. One of the officers, who had seen thousands of Zulus in Cape Colony,[9] remarked rather carelessly, "There are Zulus who are better developed physically than this chap, captain. You should see some of the Zulu warriors if you want to see perfectly developed men. This chap is a Yoruba Negro, and if you know anything about Negroes in Africa, you must know that the Yoruba Negroes are among the best scholars in Africa." The young man was now almost within speaking distance of the group and the captain, excusing himself from his companions, advanced toward and greeted him with a "How do you do, my friend?" The young man returned the greeting with "Quite well, I thank you. How are you, sir?"

The captain had not expected this kind of English from a half-naked "African savage," as Negroes in Africa are called by complacent egotists in the white race, who imagine that civilization, which, as Da Rocha[10] says, is a relative term, began and will end with them.

The captain looked the surprise he felt. The young African, noticing his embarrassment, added: "You seem surprised, sir, because I answered you in English. I speak very good English. Is it not so?"

"Oh, yes, yes," responded the captain, recovering from his shock. "I was wondering where you learned our tongue. Your people have a language of their own, have they not?"

"Certainly, sir," replied the young man with a polite bow. "There are as many languages among Africans as there are tribes, and we sometimes add to them. I speak and write the Yoruba language, that is my tribal language. I also speak and write French, German, Arabic, Italian and English."[11]

7

"W-w-why, where did you manage to learn to speak and write all those languages, young man?" asked the now thoroughly surprised captain. "Come aboard my ship. I want to talk to you. You really interest me." Addressing his late companions he begged them to excuse him while he interviewed the young black man, which they willingly did.

The captain repeated his invitation to the young man to visit him in his cabin, but he seeming to hesitate, and the captain, divining what he was revolving over in his mind, quickly assured him that he would not carry him off in his ship. The young man smiled faintly and followed the captain into the little naphtha launch to his handsomely appointed cabin in the ship, in midstream, where he entertained that worthy until the stars began to shed their lustre on the earth with the story of his life.

Captain De Forrest, as soon as the young man had seated himself in the comfortable arm-chair which he had placed for him, sat himself down in a big leather rocker directly opposite his visitor, and taking from his coat pocket a well-filled cigar case, opened it and offered the young black man one of the big black Havana cigars which it contained.

"I thank you for your kindness, sir," said Mojola—Mojola Okukenu[12] was the name of the young African—but I do not smoke or use tobacco in any form."

"Drink?" queried the captain.

"I am glad to be able to say, sir, that that is another habit to which I am not addicted."

"Well, my young man, I wish I could truthfully say as much as that, but unfortunately I cannot," and removing the stopper from a well-filled decanter which sat on the little round table, he filled his glass with rare old Madeira, which he quaffed only as a connoisseur quaffs an old vintage with a bouquet and a history. Setting his glass down the captain lighted one of the big black cigars which lay on the table and then settled back in his rocker in an easy attitude, a picture of contentment, and requested Mojola to tell him something about himself.

"I do not know that my story will specially interest you, sir," said

Mojola, "but since you have asked it I will tell you as much of it as modesty and time will permit." He began:

Mojola Okukenu's Story.

"When I was quite a small boy I attended, with my brother who is now in America,[13] a mission school which had been established by some white men who came from England in the village in which I was born, in Yorubaland.

"I went to this school regularly for two years and learned while a pupil there to speak English fluently and write it with considerable facility. My teacher, seeing my aptitude for letters, encouraged me in every way, and as time grew he persuaded my father, then a very old man, to consent to my going to England with him, whither he was going to recuperate his health. The climate of Africa is death to white men, and except in South Africa, where the temperatures are very similar to those of some portions of Europe, they cannot remain more than six months or a year without showing the bad effects of the tropical climate upon their health. So that for self-protection they are forced to make bi-annual voyages to England, or Scotland, or Germany, and if not too far gone physically, return and resume their work, but more of them go home to die than to return.

"My father thought long over this request of my teacher to take me to the white man's country, and in three weeks from the time it was made he gave his consent, only on the promise that I was to be brought back or sent back within a year from the day of sailing and at the expense of my teacher. This promise was made in writing, sealed, signed and delivered to my father in the presence of the head men of our tribe, which being done, I was placed in charge of my future guardian and protector, who was to sail to England on the steamship 'Crown Princess,' due to arrive within the next ten days.

"When my brother Sadipe learned that we were to be separated for a whole year it made him quite sad at heart, and on the morning that

9

we took ship for England he showed the strength of the great love he bore me by restraining his tears until just as the great vessel lifted anchor and was getting up steam to make the long journey to England. With his hand in mine we stood on deck gazing into each other's eyes for a moment. Finally he broke the silence, saying: 'Brother Mojola, you are going to a strange land and I feel that we are never to meet again on this earth. I am going to America. Good-bye, my dear brother. May the God of races keep His strong arm of protection around us and make us both instruments for good in His hands.' As he said these words he burst into tears, and we embraced each other, both now weeping as though our hearts would break.

"The deckhands and sailors were busy getting on board the cargo, which was being brought to the ship in canoes by 'boys' and hoisted on deck by ropes. There was a huge pile of all sorts of things on the beach to be placed on board, and the captain was busy giving orders to the workers on board, and everybody, both those ashore and those aboard, were as busy as they could well be. I told Sadipe when he had recovered from his fit of depression that I really did not want to go to England, but that our father wanted me to go with my teacher and learn more about the white man in his native land. He told me that I would never be happy there, separated from kindred and friends, 'but go, Mojola, and make the most of your opportunities. It may be that you will be the better for it,' and so, brother Sadipe, I bowed to the will of our good father, confident that he knew what was best for me. We both agreed that it was perhaps a wise thing for me to go to England and, much as I disliked the long journey, I felt that there was some special providence in it. My brother and I stood at the rail on the upper deck and talked of many things until the ship was loosed from her moorings, and when the whistle blew the last signal a native canoe came alongside the ship and he was lowered into it and was taken ashore.

"I stood on the after-deck of the great vessel and saw him safely land, and I remained there and watched him and exchanged signals with him until he faded from view.

The Black Sleuth

"The good ship on which we journeyed reached Liverpool within the time she was scheduled to arrive, and on the evening of the day of our arrival we set out for London, our objective. My teacher had letters of credit on the great firm of Wellborne & Coverdale, which he presented, but owing to a clerical error he was obliged to wait until a cable could be sent to Lagos, West Africa, to correct it. It was one of those clerical blunders which even the best of clerks sometimes make. This clerk had forgotten in his haste to write in the name of the bearer of the letter, and it had been necessary for Messrs. Wellborne & Coverdale to ascertain to whom they were really to pay over the £300 for which the letter called. The British Consul at Lagos satisfied them that the letter was in the right hands, and that the money should be paid bearer. The money, all in crisp Bank of England notes, was paid to my teacher and we took a compartment in an afternoon steam car for the great metropolis. I had never before ridden in a steam car and you may well imagine my feelings and sensations on this my initial overland trip on wheels propelled by steam."

"Got scared, eh?" queried the captain, blowing a big mouthful of smoke in the direction of Mojola, which he skillfully dodged.

"I do not think, sir, that I ever was afraid or 'scared,' as you call it, of anybody or anything except once in my life, and that was when I first saw a man of your race, who came to our country wearing European clothes, the like of which we had never before seen. My people declared it to be their belief that he was the devil, an evil spirit sent to persecute and torment us. We Africans, I must here add, associate the white man with the prince of evil and all that is wicked and bad.[14] No, I was not scared nor afraid, but I was filled with amazement, wonder, surprise at the speed of the iron horse and the inventive skill and genius of the white man, who had constructed this wonderful machine which was bearing us through space almost with the swiftness of the wind. Wonderful, wonderful, I kept saying to myself as I gazed out of the window of the car and saw, as I then supposed, the houses and trees and other inanimate objects moving speedily through space."[15]

"I want to know about yourself, young man, and where you learned to speak English so well and the other languages which you tell me you can speak and write," said the captain eagerly.

"If you will permit me to summarize my story, sir, I think I can satisfy you on those points. I never had any one to teach me the languages I speak other than my own and what you call English except nature, and I was and tried always to be a conscientious and tireless student. I hold that there is nothing within the scope of human endeavor which a resolute man may not accomplish if he so wills. But I must tell my story in my own way, sir. If you wish to hear me further I will proceed."

"Go on! go on! I beg pardon for interrupting you," said the captain.

Continuing, Mojola said: "When we alighted from our compartment in London that afternoon

(*To be continued.*)

CHAPTER III

"We were met at the station by quite a number of the personal friends of my teacher and a small delegation of the members of the church which had sent him out to Africa to take up the 'white man's burden' of civilizing, Christianizing and educating the heathen of that 'benighted land.'

"Due notice, of course, had been given of my coming, and when I arrived in London I became the cynosure of all eyes and was paraded and exhibited in the churches of this particular denomination as a specimen of the work turned out by the missionaries sent out to Africa by its Foreign Mission Board. I was called on at missionary meetings to read portions of Scriptures in my native tongue, and as I had a fair voice and understood music to some extent, I was always asked to sing some one or other of the white man's (meaningless to us) gospel hymns in the Yoruba tongue.

"At the close of these meetings the people would crowd around me and ply me with all sorts of foolish questions about Africa and say many foolish things about the Africans which disclosed their crass ignorance of my country and its people, as well as their overweening conceit. All of these things disgusted me more than I can tell you, sir, for in my young mind I had conceived the idea that your race was representative of the highest intelligence, and that modesty and good breeding were its chief characteristics in matters religious, but this experience disillusioned me; its pharisaism really disgusted me."

The captain gazed steadily at the bold young African, who was all unconscious of the force of his words, winced and turned uneasily in his chair. Continuing, Mojola said:

"My observation of things spiritual and temporal in England convinced me that I could never adapt myself to English ideas or customs, or accept with a sincere heart the white man's conception of the religion taught and practiced by Jesus of Nazareth, of whom we in Yorubaland have at least heard something.

"All that I had observed during the first few weeks of my sojourn in England impressed me deeply with the idea that there was more sham and hypocrisy than reality in the thing he is trying to inject into the African and other so-called heathen[16]—the hollowness of their professions of brotherhood was to me so transparent I determined that I would, on the first opportunity that presented itself, return to my own country.[17]

"In the course of a few months I was able to do this, and I do not now regret that I left the 'centre of civilization' and returned to the land of 'darkness and barbarism,' as Africa is ignorantly styled by those who do not know better, and who are accustomed from long practice to reason with their prejudices."

"You are a pretty plain speaker, young man," said the captain, who was quite red in the face.

"Truth should always be spoken plainly, sir," said Mojola. "Before your race had a civilization or a religion, mine was, and from it your race has borrowed and stolen all that was best and most useful in art, science, religion, letters, politics and government, from which you have evolved what you proudly term Anglo-Saxon civilization. Intelligent Africans laugh at your complacent egotism."[18]

"Umph!" muttered the captain. "What do you do here?" said he, trying to change the subject. "I mean what opportunities have you here for using the knowledge you acquired in England?"

"I am teaching my people the true Gospel—that God is no respecter of persons.[19] The knowledge I acquired in England is only useful for purposes of comparison: for, believe me, sir, we sift it as occasion requires, and it sometimes suffers by comparison. We in Africa are not nearly so dumb, ignorant, nor benighted as the white man seems to believe us to be."

"Umph!" grunted the captain, looking askance at the bold young African, who, without apparently noticing this interruption, went on to say:

"The Yorubas are one of the most advanced African tribes. We have the Bible translated from the original Greek and Hebrew texts by our own native scholars, a grammar, hymn books, a history of Yorubaland by native historians and many other evidences showing that we are not as benighted nor as barbarous as white people with the missionary fever and itching palms represent us to be." This was too much for the captain; he had heard enough. Rising from his comfortable armchair, he advanced toward the young man. Espying a small gunnysack on the floor of the cabin nearly under the chair in which Mojola sat, he asked him what it contained, assuming that he was selling *curios*.

"Oh, they are merely specimens of rock; I am very fond of geology, sir, and I sometimes gather these specimens along the seashore and other places in my wanderings to illustrate my lectures to our Yoruba boys." The captain looked his astonishment. Here, in the heart of Africa, Africa which he had been taught to believe was the home of a wild and barbarous and heathenish people who ate good, white missionaries three times a day and each other, occasionally, according to the missionary reports and friendly newspapers.[20] He was standing face to face with one of these heathen and barbarians who was better educated than himself, who spoke purer English, and who had a better general idea of books than he, and a more analytical mind. His Caucasian pride and conceit, however, would not allow him to discover his mental deficiencies to this half-naked black man, and despite his short comings he felt his superiority over a man whom his own heart told him was his master in the force that wins—brains.

While he was thus musing, Mojola had opened the gunny-sack and spread the specimens on the table at which they sat. The captain's experienced eye detected among them one that struck him as being more than a specimen. It was a flinty substance about the size of an English walnut. The captain picked it up, ran his eye over it critically and laid it down carelessly, but kept his eye on it. He examined other specimens; one resembling a moonstone and almost perfectly round excited his admiration. He asked its name, and received the answer; and, as if forgetting that he had once examined the larger specimen, he picked it up again and fondled it. The young African, who had been watching him closely, and observing that he was particularly *interested* in that specimen, vouchsafed the information that that was a diamond in the rough.

"A diamond!" exclaimed the captain in a tone that betrayed the workings of his mind.

The young African, with aggravating nonchalance, calmly assured him that it was, and that they were frequently to be met with in the section of the country from which he came, some of them even larger than this.[21] The captain's eyes bulged out. The wily young African had awakened in the avaricious white man before him the spirit which had led thousands of his race to seek fame and fortune—mostly fortune— in the "dark continent," which, with bitter irony, is not inappropriately called the graveyard of the grasping nations of the earth.

Mojola smiled as he watched the face of the man who had been so much interested in the story of his life, and he read his innermost thoughts.

"Will you sell me this specimen, young man? I want it and will pay you a good price for it."[22]

CHAPTER IV

The eager tone of the captain's voice caused the young African to smile as he looked up from the table over which he was engaged in placing in the little gunny-sack the remaining specimens which he had strewn upon it for the inspection of his host, and he answered in the soft tones peculiar to the people of Yorubaland: "If it is of any value to you, sir, you may have it. I can easily find another and perhaps a better one."

The captain's eyes almost popped out of their sockets at the words "a better one." Could it be possible, thought he, that there was still a better diamond on earth than his experienced eye told him this one was? "Oh, no, no, no; I—I—I—I—want to, I must pay you something for it. It would not be right to take it as a gift," said he, more excitedly than the occasion seemed to warrant.

"Very well," said the young African, "have your way about it, sir. We Africans do not set our hearts on the possession of money. It is the cheapest thing we have amongst us, except the air we breathe and the water we drink. Our currency is made in nature's mint and is stamped by a 'divinity that shapes our ends.'[23] We use cowry shells, and about a thousand of them would equal in value six of your English pennies."

"Your millionaires began saving about the year one, didn't they?" queried the captain.

"We have no millionaires among our people, sir. The accumulation and hoarding of wealth is an invention of the white man, and Africa is just now the centre of his activity. He is plundering Africa like a buccaneer in quest of gold and diamonds and ivory, and he returns to Europe or America broken in health to die, or perchance he dies in the wilds of my country in the mad struggle to possess himself of ill-gotten gains.

"Take the late Cecil Rhodes.[24] Where was there a more grasping, soulless creature than he? He accumulated millions on millions and lived like a king amongst us, but he died without realizing his dream of empire.[25] He, like all who have preceded him or who are now fol-lowing, or may hereafter follow his example of plundering the Africans in the name of civilization and religion, will fail ingloriously in any at-tempt to establish in the black man's country a white civilization or to reverse the decree of the Almighty.[26]

"Africa is for the African,[27] and the white man can never perma-nently abide within its boundaries. The African will ultimately enjoy the fruits of the white man's persistent labors in developing the coun-try, and [often the white man] has obligingly died, leaving some other misguided white man to take up his world.[28] It is an old story, sir. For a thousand years the nations of the earth have been casting lots for the possession of Africa, but Africa possesses them, as their bleaching bones in vale and forest mutely testify. God does not intend that the white man shall possess our land. It is a 'Rubicon' he cannot cross.[29] No matter how many nations partition Africa, Africa will still be Africa.[30]

"Africans will absorb and assimilate your learning, will study your system of government, and will analyze and dissect whatever is best and most useful to them in your civilization, whatever is rational and reasonable in your religion, whatever is practical and just in your le-gal jurisprudence, and then construct her own code of morals and ethics for use against the time when 'Ethiopia shall suddenly stretch forth her hands unto God.' She will be equipped with all the learning and wisdom and knowledge of all the races of the earth with whom she has come in contact, and will be ready to take her proper place among the nations. She has no fears as to her future. Her star is in the ascendant. She stands upon the threshold of a future pregnant with hope and big with magnificent possibilities."[31]

As Mojola Okukenu uttered these words, Captain De Forrest, who had lost interest in the fat cigar which he had been smoking and which now lay beside his big, fat right arm, which was lazily resting on the round table in his cabin, gazed in astonishment and amazement at the speaker and finally uttered a deep sigh expressive of his feelings. In a moment or two his tongue found speech and he said, "Young man, I have listened with interest to your story and I have been profitably entertained and highly instructed by your display of learning and wisdom. You have talents and abilities of no mean order, and you have the gift of putting your thoughts in clear, cogent and forceful English. Not every man is as well qualified as you to give voice to his thoughts in such clear, pungent, and terse language. Your story has most thoroughly convinced me that there is no difference between men in the republic of intellect; that the black man's brain is just as capable of higher development as a white man's under proper conditions." The Captain looked as wise and solemn as an owl after admitting this Solomonic (?) gem.

The young African replied, "That is hardly a compliment, sir. God did not create black men or white men, but MAN, out of the loins of whom came all the varieties of men who now inhabit the earth—equal in the beginning, and equal always before Him.

"Opportunity and environment are the standards by which all men should be judged, not color. It is no compliment to the Negro to tell him that he is as good as a white man, for that presupposes that the white man is a superior being, which is not true. His opportunities and environment have done for him exactly what they would have done for the black man similarly placed.

"Whenever the Negro has had fair opportunities, he has always shown himself equal to them, and in my country there are many men of learning and ability, equal and in many respects superior to those who have been more fortunately placed.

19

"Color is no criterion of superiority or the lack of it, sir. All brains have the same color; all blood is red.

"Your Scottish bard, Robert Burns, has expressed my thoughts in these words:

"'The rank is but the guinea's stamp;
A man's a man for a' that and a' that.'[32]

"And now, sir. I must beg you to permit me to say good evening to you, for I have remained aboard your ship much longer than I had expected."

"Oh! You needn't be in a hurry, young man; you are excellent company and I enjoy your conversation immensely."

"I thank you for that, sir," answered the young African. "I trust I have talked to some purpose."

"You have converted me and while you were talking so earnestly and eloquently a few moments ago, I registered a vow that the black man will ever find in me an unflinching friend, and now I give you my hand, my young friend, in pledge of friendship to your race. My purse, my house, my heart will always be open to any worthy Negro in trouble or need."[33]

"Then our meeting has really been prolific of good?" asked Mojola.

"It has," replied the Captain. "I have learned more about the Negro today than I ever knew before or ever dreamed was true. You belong to a great race, and you have shown me why it is a great race. When I was a boy at Sunday school I often read, without understanding it, a passage in the Bible which ran something like this: 'He that is least among you will be greatest.'[34] I know now what that passage means."

"I am happy and gratified," said Mojola, "to know that I have been the means of leading you to see the African in a new light, and I am glad to number you among the true friends of my countrymen. And now, Captain, again I must say good evening. I have enjoyed the meeting with you, and I assure you the benefits have been mutual."

The Black Sleuth

The young man shook the Captain warmly by the hand and, stepping to the door of the cabin, was soon on his way down the rope ladder on the side of the great ship, where he was met by one of the numerous "boys" who had previously been ordered by Captain De Forrest to come out and take his visitor ashore in a native boat, and he was soon lost in the shadows of the evening.

"Most remarkable young Negro I ever met," mused the Captain, picking up his cigar and lighting it. "We whites can never keep down a race that produces men of that stamp." He strolled leisurely aft, and sat down in a big steamer chair, smoked and thought of many things.

The skies in Africa in autumn are beautiful to behold. The stars seem to be nearer to earth than they do in other parts of the world. Their coruscations are like those of a newly cut diamond in a setting of opal and gold. The captain shifted his chair to a point where he could sweep the horizon with his big glass, and he gazed at the stars and thought of Mojola for two or three hours, and then retired to his comfortable bed, where he courted the god Morpheus,[35] with a particularly strong cigar.

(*To be continued.*)

CHAPTER V

Six days after the departure of Mojola for England, Sadipe Oku-kenu, his brother, who was three years his junior, took passage on an American sailing vessel for the United States. He had pleaded earnestly with his old father for permission to go, and he had yielded, though somewhat reluctantly, to his importunities. The name of the vessel on which he sailed was the "Water Witch." Her captain was a down-easter, and, like most of the men from that part of America, he had a great deal of genuine sympathy for the Negro. He, too, had urged the boy's father to let him make the voyage, saying that it would be a liberal education to him and that the knowledge thus gained would be useful to him in the future. He promised to put the boy in a good school and to have him properly and carefully educated, so that when he reached his majority he could return to his native land and use his talents for the uplift of his "benighted race." This philosophical observation caused the shrewd old African to smile. His knowledge of white men, gained from dealing with them on the coast, taught him that conceit was not among the least of their accomplishments. "Nature has been kind to them," he mused, " in the bestowal of her gifts, and this white man actually believes that his race can teach my race something. He either forgets, or does not know, that the very Bible he professes to believe came from the East, not from the West, and that we Africans had a great deal more to do with its promulgation than he is aware of."

The Black Sleuth

These were some of the thoughts that ran through his mind while he sat on his stool facing the white man who awaited his answer about his boy Sadipe. Rising abruptly and pacing up and down for several moments, he stopped directly in front of the captain and said:

"You say you will send my boy to a good school in America?"

"Oh, yes," answered the Captain; "I will take him with me to Maine and place him in charge of my sister, who is very fond of black people. She will prepare him for school, and when he is ready to enter will send him to a Negro college, where they will make a doctor or preacher or lawyer out of him."

"Are there any Christians in your country?"

"Why, certainly, my good man, America is the most Christian country on the globe. We contribute more money, verily, to civilize and Christianize the heathen in foreign lands than almost any other nation on earth. You could not send Sadipe to a better place than America; it is a progressive country, and black men there enjoy the same rights as white men."

"But why do you say you will send my boy to a Negro college when he is prepared to go to one? Why do you have Negro colleges if all men have the same rights in your country and are all equal? Why do you thus separate the races?"

"Oh! That is the custom in my country; the black people have their own schools and churches, and they would not come to ours."

"Then the black man is superior to the white man; is that it?"

"Well—er—er—hardly that. You see, we have a peculiar condition of affairs in America. The blacks were once in slavery to the white race and are considered to be not quite equal to them in morals and intelligence, due to their former condition. We have a very kind feeling in our hearts for the black people and we are helping them through our churches and schools of learning to become self-respecting and useful citizens. Politically they have all the rights that white citizens enjoy and many of them hold offices of great trust and responsibility."

"And yet you are divided in your schools and churches, where perfect equality should exist?" asked the wily old African, who was not quite as green as he looked.

"Tell me," he said, straightening himself up to his full height, "is a man-stealer in your country regarded as an honorable man, and are men-killers respected in your country? I have heard that you Americans have stolen thousands of my people from their homes here in Africa to make them slaves, and that since freedom came to them you kill them by burning them at the stake and lynching them, as you call it. Are these white men superior to black men?"

Captain Barnard looked at the old African quizzically and intently as he was speaking, as if trying to read his very soul. Here in the very heart of Africa he was standing face to face with one of her sable sons, who was discussing with him a question of ethics that made him blush for shame for the "most Christian nation on earth."

A man whose appearance concealed more than it revealed; a deep, cool-headed old Negro with a logical mind, who was putting questions to him that stung his pride and made him ashamed to own the name "American."

His answers to these questions were such only as an honest, God-fearing white American could give them. He said:

"We do not, in America, regard men-stealers and men-killers as honorable men, but as thieves and murderers; their crimes have disgraced the American name and made it a byword and hissing among the nations, and our children and our children's children will bear the stigma and suffer the consequences of these crimes against God and man for generations yet unborn."

The Captain uttered the words with considerable feeling and emphasis, and there was no mistaking his sincerity.

The elder Okukenu listened respectfully to the white man, and when he had finished he extended his hand and said:

"I am willing, sir, that my boy Sadipe shall accompany you in your voyage to America. I wish him to go that he may see for himself how the white man in America lives. I have no fear about his not returning to his home here in Africa. The Okukenus will not submit to oppression or injustice in any form, no matter where they are, and if Sadipe is not treated well in your country he will find a way to get back to the land of his fathers. I give to both of you my blessings and my prayers for a safe voyage. I am willing to trust him to your care, for your speech shows you to be a good man, a God-fearing man, and men who fear and reverence God can do no wrong."

The day after this remarkable interview between the Captain and the elder Okukenu, exactly at high noon, the "Water Witch" lifted anchor and was soon speeding away on her long journey to the Western Hemisphere.

"Unless above himself he doth erect himself,
How poor a thing is man."[36]

The finest thing in the human life is its constant struggle toward something better—something noble.

The little black boy who stood on the forward deck of the "Water Witch," as she rode majestically upon the bosom of the placid waters, was destined for a better fate than he had ever dreamed of. The stars in their courses were conspiring to make his future as brilliant, as successful. Sadipe was a boy of uncommon native and acquired abilities for one of his age. He was of a lively temperament, high-spirited and manly in bearing, quick-witted and apt. He was passionately fond of books, and, young as he was—he was just turning nineteen[37]—he spoke two native dialects and was quite familiar with Arabic. He could read the Koran understandingly, and had memorized many passages from it, which was not an uncommon performance for boys of his age, and even younger, who were constantly thrown in contact with the followers of Mohammed.

His father was of that faith, and five times each day in the year he and his household reverently prostrated themselves before Him whom Jean Paul Richter declares "is the holiest among the mighty and the mightiest among the holy."[38]

Sadipe stood unconsciously upon the threshold of a future pregnant

with mighty possibilities,[39] and as they subsequently unfolded themselves to him he proved himself equal to every emergency that arose,
as the sequel will show.

(*To be continued.*)

CHAPTER VI

Of the details of Sadipe's experience after his arrival in America we will say nothing further than that Captain Barnard treated him with the utmost consideration en voyage, and on his arrival at his home in Maine (or rather the home of his good sister, for the Captain was a typical sea rover) he and that good lady conspired to make the young African feel as much at home as they knew how.

The Captain's sister, Mrs. Tabitha Pelham, was a motherly sort of a women, kind-hearted, indulgent and gentle of manner. She took the greatest interest in Sadipe. From their first meeting she liked his face, and told her brother that the boy was above the average of his race in intelligence and that his manner and speech indicated that there was really something in him. She was able to reach these conclusions from the fact that she had for more than twenty years taught a school for boys in an adjoining town[40] and knew somewhat of boys.

She accordingly began to prepare her young African charge for the business of real life. His natural aptitude was in his favor, and he learned rapidly. He was particularly adept in mathematics and Latin, and he had a taste for history which was encouraged by his patron.

The English classics were also a favorite study with him, and in these he displayed a breadth of mind and a range of vision which not only astonished but greatly pleased his instructor. He was eager to acquire a knowledge of French and German, and to gratify his wishes

Mrs. Pelham, after a few weeks, employed a teacher of these languages to come to the house two evenings in the week and instruct her young charge in the mysteries of these languages. His knowledge of Latin greatly facilitated the work of his instructor, and helped both the teacher and the taught to make progress. Like most Negroes, he was passionately fond of music, good music, and in the fullness of time Mrs. Pelham employed a music teacher, Prof. Rogers of the conservatory, who taught him how to perform on the pianoforte, the young man going to the conservatory two evenings a week when his daily tasks were done. He was regarded as a sort of prodigy by some of the villagers, who had views as to the intellectual capacity of the black man. They could not comprehend how a black boy could advance so rapidly in studies which required two, sometimes four years for white boys to master.

Here was a black boy who within less than a year had become proficient in the fundamentals of learning and had learned to speak and write Latin, French and German, mastered the rudiments of natural philosophy, knew the English poets and was not a bad performer on the piano. They shook their heads and asked each other, Will wonders never cease?

But these good and well-meaning villagers did not know that the race to which this "boy" belonged was born to scholarship; that the tribe in Africa with which he was identified is, with the exception of the Fantis,[41] the most intellectual tribe in all Africa. Had they known these facts they would not have marveled.

Sadipe had come to America to learn things, and he was determined to learn all he could.

After eighteen months' hard and conscientious study, and having exhausted good Mrs. Pelham's stock of information (for she confessed that she could go no further with him), he was ready for college. At the beginning of the fall term of the Eckington College for Colored Youth he found himself the possessor of a scholarship—the joint gift of Mrs. Pelham and Col. Amos Otis, President of the Sago National Bank, who was greatly interested in the boy and as proud of him as Mrs. Pelham, who showed her admiration for his fine abilities in many ways.

After much preparation he was sent off to Eckington College well supplied with strong letters to prominent men of his own race living in the vicinity of the school, who were advised of his phenomenal talents and urged to show him the hospitality worthy of a young man so well favored by nature. Finally on Saturday morning of that week he took leave of his kind patron, Mrs. Pelham, and set his face toward Eckington College, in that far Southern State, traveling as a first-class passenger until he reached the capital city of the nation, which is sandwiched between two of the old slave states, Maryland and Virginia, and where race prejudice is almost thick enough to cut with a knife.

Here, in the home of the President of the United States, the seat of power, where the laws which govern the country are made, where equality of citizenship is proclaimed in the national Congress, and where there were more Negroes of varying shades and conditions than Sadipe had ever before seen in America, he received the first great shock of the many which he was to experience on the two days' journey before him. His train arriving late in Washington, his journey was delayed several hours, and he strolled out of the Pennsylvania Station, up Sixth street, into Pennsylvania avenue and meandered leisurely toward the great white-domed Capitol, upon whose highest point the Goddess of Liberty stood in mock seriousness keeping guard (?) over the liberties and rights of the people. Meeting a black man, he asked the name of the building and the meaning of the big statue on the top. Being told, he jotted down in the notebook given him by Mrs. Pelham the name of the building and the Goddess misnamed "Liberty." Continuing his journey, he brought up at the Peace Monument[42] at First Street and Pennsylvania avenue. He read the legend at its base and noted it in his book, and then, retracing his steps, soon found himself again in the station just as the guard was crying "All aboard! This way for the train South."

He started for the gate and attempted to enter. The ticket-taker, a coarse, gruff, red-haired Irishman, stopped him. "Where's your ticket, old man? Yez can't go troo widout showing yure ticket." Sadipe gave him a withering look of scorn and stepped out of the line. Going over to a window, he searched his pockets for the coveted pasteboard, which he had securely placed in an envelope with the cash given him by Mrs. Pelham. Carefully replacing the envelope in an inner pocket and fastening the pocket with the large safety pin which Mrs. Pelham had also given him, to make sure of it staying there, he returned to the gate and presented his ticket. The Irishman scanned it critically before punching it, punched it and slapped Sadipe on the back, saying, "There's yure train, old man; step lively now."

"You are an insolent, impudent brute; how dare you strike me?" said Sadipe, who was boiling with indignation at the coarse and vulgar and insolent action of the uniformed underling. "I have a great notion to slap your face!" said the spunky boy.[43] A gentleman who had witnessed the conduct of the ticket-taker and heard the objectionable remarks which offended Sadipe here came forward and said: "Young man, this fellow has wantonly and grossly insulted you, and you should report him at once to the company. If you will give me your name I myself will do so, and state what I saw and heard. I am a stockholder in this company and am sure that the rules of the management require that all employees shall at least be civil to its patrons."

While Sadipe and his newmade and unknown friend were thus talking the Southern train drew out from the station and left him. The gentleman consulted a timetable and told him that there would be another train at 12:03. Stepping into the telegraph office in the station, he wired the President of Eckington College that he had missed his train and would take the 12:03. His newfound friend and he then sought the office of the superintendent, which was upstairs, where they jointly complained of the action of the insolent employee at the gate, and that person was sent for by the superintendent and confronted with the charges made. He made an abject apology for his bad manner, and was warned that if another complaint was made against him his name would be changed from Michael to Dennis.

Having come off victor in shock number one, Sadipe was given shock number two at exactly 12:15. He was now on the train going South. It was rapidly nearing the Virginia line, where the metamorphosis of the colored people begins, when the conductor, with a scowl on his face, approached him and took his ticket. "Here," he said, gruffly, "you belong in the darkies' kyar; this heah kyar is for white folks only; you must git, old man; your kyar is the last but one in the rear; step lively, thar!" Sadipe could not believe his senses. He was nonplussed, and he was also very angry, and he decided to fight. How, we shall see in the next chapter.[44]

CHAPTER VII[45]

Remembering that he had purchased, as he believed, a first-class ticket to his destination in the South, he made haste to apprise this ungentlemanly minion of a soulless corporation that he would stand on his rights as he understood them, as a first-class passenger.

"Yo' will, eh!" sneered the conductor, and with that remark he stepped into the next car, whence he returned in a few minutes with two able-bodied Negro porters. When the trio had gotten well into the car the white passengers, anticipating a lot of fun, and possibly some trouble, gathered in groups in the aisles and stood up in their seats to see "the Nigger," as some of them expressed it, bounced into "Nigger heaven," as the Jim Crow cars are sometimes called. Opening wide the door of the car leading to the filthy and foul-smelling sweat-box reserved for Negro passengers, and with the bravado and swagger of the bully that his looks proclaimed him, the blustering underling commanded the colored porters, one of whom was decidedly black, while the other was quite fair, to "yank that fresh coon into the Nigro kyar," pointing toward Sadipe, who was now boiling over with indignation. His African blood was at white heat, and he was the more incensed because of the significance of this fresh insult—the bringing into the car of two men of his own color and race to further degrade and humiliate him at the bidding of a vulgar, ignorant and foul-mouthed white man. He sat perfectly still in his seat and refused to budge.

The Black Sleuth

"Be lively thar, now!" roared the big brute. "Yo' all take that Nigra out'n this kyar. Yo' know ez well ez I do that he ain't got no business in this heah kyar. This kyar's for white folk!" With this remark he glanced toward the groups of white passengers gathered around as if looking for a nod or a smile of approval of his superserviceable efforts to relieve them from the disgrace and humiliation of riding in a steam "kyar with a Nigra."

Sadipe now arose, and with a look of anger he said quietly but firmly: "Conductor, I defy either you or these black men whom you have brought here to drag me into a filthy car, which you call the 'Nigra kyar,' to lay the weight of a finger on me. I shall not leave this car unless you or they kill me." And he said this so finely, so determinedly and with such cool, calm deliberateness that the passengers (most of whom were Northerners en route to Florida) applauded the plucky black boy.

One of the porters, a strapping, handsome-faced black fellow, evidently ashamed of his part in the little comedy, said: "I did not come in here with the intention of forcing you out of this car, mister. I am a servant of this company, and I am expected to obey orders; but this is one order *I will not obey,* and I realize what a refusal to do so means."

The conductor glared at the manly porter and remarked: "Mr. Nigra, this is yo last run over this heah road."

"There are other roads," joined the porter, "and they do not lead to hell." With this, he turned on his heel and went back to his car.

The other porter, a freckle-faced, sandy-haired specimen of the genus African, was then ordered to take "thet Nigra out." He also refused. He did not seem to like the determined look in Sadipe's eye, and then, too, neither he nor the conductor were quite sure that he was not "loaded."

The blustering white bully being thus thwarted, made, or pretended to, some notes in a blank book and left the car. The passengers snickered and resumed their seats. Sadipe changed his position and thought of many things.

There was one interested witness to all that we have here recorded—a white man, evidently a man of influence and culture. Just before the train pulled into Gordonsville, Va., he took his bag and other belongings and came into the seat where Sadipe sat musing and brooding over his experiences. "Excuse me," he said; "may I sit here with you? I am afraid you are going to have some trouble, and I have resolved to befriend you, if you will permit me."

Sadipe thanked him heartily for his kind interest in him and assured him that he was quite welcome to remain. The gentleman stooped down, and, opening a small handbag, took out a six-shooter and deftly passed it to Sadipe, who understood and quickly placed the weapon in the outer pocket of his great-coat.

The two then engaged in conversation and introduced themselves to each other. The white gentleman passed his card to Sadipe. It read: "General R. M. De Mortie, U.S.A." Sadipe wrote his name on a blank card, "Sadipe Okukenu, West Africa." The white gentleman told Sadipe that he was from the West, where he commanded one of the crack Negro regiments, and that he regarded Negro soldiers as the bravest and best in the service. He said he had experienced enough with them in the Civil War and in the Indian wars to satisfy him that there were no braver men in the service.

While the two men were thus engaged in conversation some of the other passengers became interested and moved up and down the aisle of the car at intervals, as if to catch some word of the earnest conversation in which they were engaged, and they exchanged meaning looks with each other. This General De Mortie observing, he lowered his tone somewhat, and, changing the subject when the next eavesdropper strolled leisurely down to the ice-water tank, he asked Sadipe for his name and place of birth.

"Oh!" he said; "then you are a British subject. How long have you been in this country?"

Sadipe told him that he had lived here almost two years.

The spy heard these words; they were meant for his ears. Returning to his seat at the upper end of the car, he evidently communicated what he heard to his companions, with whom he engaged in whispered conversation for several minutes.

"My young friend," said General De Mortie, "we are now nearing Gordonsville. That cowardly rascal of a conductor may go out when the train stops and bring in a lot of thugs and plug-uglies to force you into the Negro car. If he does, and they attempt to interfere with you, shoot the first scoundrel that lays hands on you. I will take care of the others."

Sadipe felt in his pocket to make sure that the weapon was still there, and, looking the General in the eye, he said: "I had already resolved, sir, to defend myself, and I assure you that I am not afraid to die, if need be, in defense of my honor and manhood."

"Well said," replied the General. "Here we are; this is Gordonsville. Keep your eyes open and your hand on the trigger."

The train came to a standstill. From the window at which Sadipe sat he saw a motley crowd of station loafers, lean, lank, hungry-looking poor whites; Negro men and women mingling with the crowd of passengers, who were making their way to the train, [were] trying to dispose of fried chicken and green-apple pies. The poor whites were seated on boxes of freight, barrels, trunks, anything that would support their lazy bodies. Across the way from the station were a half dozen or more poor whites astride a fence, chewing tobacco and whittling with their jackknives pieces of pine wood. Presently the baggage smashers came along with their four-wheeled trucks and dislodged some of the sitters on the station platform and gathered up the boxes and trunks and barrels and transferred them to the baggage car.

These stood up and yawned, and then moved their lazy, ill-clad carcases to another part of the platform, where they stood and gaped into the car windows and made remarks to each other about the passengers, who regarded them with curiosity, some of them never having seen before such an aggregation of shiftless, aimless white loafers and were manifestly ashamed of the "superior race."[46]

On the other side of the train, which was a long one, a number of colored women, with trays of fried chicken, home-made biscuits and pies of various kinds, were doing a brisk business with the hungry passengers within, and laughed gleefully at the witty sallies of their good-natured customers, who paid them liberally for their wares.

Just before the whistle blew the conductor came into Sadipe's car, with a brakeman and another white man with a forbidding countenance, and again ordered Sadipe to go to the Negro car. He did not appear to have sufficient courage to execute his own order. He was manifestly a blustering coward, and demanded that the men he had brought into the car with him should put the "Nigger" out. They started toward the seat occupied by Sadipe, and as they did so General De Mortie, who was now thoroughly angry and who sat facing Sadipe, arose and quietly informed the conductor and his accomplices that if they attempted to carry out their purposes there would certainly be trouble of a very serious kind. He handed the conductor his card and, stepping up closely to him, said something that seemed to take all of the bravado out of him, and he and his companions slunk out of the car like whipped curs.

The passengers snickered as the train pulled out of Gordonsville, and Sadipe once more found himself master of the situation. But he sustained another shock, of which mention will be made in another chapter.

(To be continued.)

CHAPTER VIII

"And the night shall be filled with music,
  And the cares that infest the day
Shall fold their tents like the Arabs,
  And silently steal away."[47]

Sadipe, vexed, tired and hungry (he could not procure any food on the train, though abundantly able to pay for it), arrived in the town where the college was located at 6:25 that evening, and the principal of the little school, which had been dignified by the name "college," came to the station to meet his distinguished pupil and to conduct him to his own residence on campus.

When the train stopped, the porter passed through the car and announced the train would stop fifteen minutes for lunch. Some of the hypercritical passengers wondered what kind of a lunch the train would eat, and tittered at the colored man's remark. General De Mortie and Sadipe went out on the station platform together, the former assisting the latter with his baggage.

The sight of a white man carrying a Negro's handbag was something of a novelty to the particular class of white people in this locality, and occasioned some comment. The two men stopped near the gate and chatted for a few moments. The general remarked to Sadipe that he had greatly enjoyed the ride from Washington, barring the annoyances from the conductor and his crowd, and told Sadipe that he was very glad to have made his acquaintance, and to have been of some help to him. Just then a tall, well-built colored man, wearing gold eyeglasses, a black suit and a silk hat, approached, and with a courteous bow asked if he was addressing Mr. Sadipe Okukenu. Sadipe assured him that he was that person and the colored man said he was the principal of the college, and had come to the station to take Mr. Okukenu to his house. They shook hands and Sadipe introduced him to General De Mortie. The three stood chatting for some moments, and while thus engaged the trainmen called out "All aboard!" and then began a scurrying of passengers to get aboard. Farewells were said hurriedly, and the train moved slowly out of the station. General De Mortie shook hands warmly with Sadipe and the college principal, and charged the former to write him in detail as soon as he had gotten his bearings, which he promised to do. The principal, taking up Sadipe's largest handbag, invited him to follow. He led the way to the main entrance to the station, where an old-fashioned family carriage stood, in charge of one of the students. Placing the handbags in the front seat, he opened the door of the ramshackle old vehicle and requested Sadipe to enter, and then entering himself, closed the door and bade the young man who acted as coachman to drive on quickly "as doubtless our friend here is hungry." There was certainly no mistake as to that, for Sadipe was genuinely hungry, not having tasted food since morning. He said he was "ravenously hungry." "Did you not bring a lunch with you," asked the principal. "No," said Sadipe. "I supposed that I would have no difficulty in purchasing all I wanted to eat on the train; I was told there was a dining-car attached." The principal looked at Sadipe and smiling pityingly said, "You are in the wrong part of the country for that sort of hospitality. Negroes who travel in this section are not permitted to enter the dining-cars on this road. They must either bring their lunches or go hungry till they reach their destination. It is too bad, Mr. Okukenu, but we have no remedy. Prejudice to color is a wicked thing, but we in this section have to suffer a great many inconveniences on account of our black faces."

The Black Sleuth

"And does this awful prejudice against black people exist in this town? Are black people proscribed against in the eating houses and hotels here?" asked Sadipe.

"Why, my dear young man, if you should enter one of the public houses here and ask for accommodation you would almost be lynched."

"What is that?" asked Sadipe in all innocence.

The principal could not suppress a smile as he answered: "Why, they would want to hang you."

"And is there no law to compel these places to serve the public?"

"They are licensed as public places, yes, but there is an unwritten law which operates against Negroes who attempt to make themselves part of the public," answered the principal.

"This is all very strange, indeed. I had no idea that human beings could be so intolerant of the rights of others, and all this in free America! I cannot understand it, sir."

"Neither can we," said the principal, "but we are obliged to submit to these things because we are helpless, and can do no better."[48]

"Awful! Awful!" said Sadipe, "I do not think I shall like this part of the country."

They had now reached the college grounds and were entering the road that led to the principal's house, a modest little Queen Anne cottage,[49] which sat on a knoll about seven hundred yards distant from the college buildings, and overlooking the campus. It was an ideal site for the home of a principal, as from his eyrie in the top story he could command a splendid view of the grounds and the gate through which students were compelled to pass in coming in or going out from the grounds. The boys were well aware of the fact that the professor had the advantage of them both day and night, and therefore played few pranks peculiar to students except when the professor was away in the North telling northern audiences what a wonderful work he was doing down South toward the moral redemption and regeneration of the colored race, and how badly he needed an endowment of $30,000 to put it on its feet, so that it could begin the work of solving on practical lines the race problem which is still with us. On these trips the professor usually remained away for six or eight weeks, depending somewhat on the state of the money market. And then the rising generation had six or eight weeks of solid fun. With the assistant in charge, a rather antiquated specimen of humanity, with no particular talent for the work entrusted to him, he was what some of the boys who still talked slang called a "good thing; dead easy."[50]

Into this cosy home Sadipe entered with his host, the principal, and was ushered into the neat little parlor, where he sat while the principal went to fetch his wife and daughter, to whom he introduced the now thoroughly hungry young man. After the usual exchange of courtesies, he was shown to the room he was to occupy for the night and left to arrange his toilet for the savory supper, the odor of which filled the halls and crept in through the keyholes of his room door. He did quick work here, divesting himself of his soiled shirt and collar, removing the surplus coal dust and cinders from his ears and face. Fifteen minutes was all the time consumed in preparing to face that supper. Descending the stairs as he had been bidden to do, he re-entered the little parlor, where he found Miss Swift and her father waiting to escort him to the dining-room, and he gladly yielded to their courteous invitation to "walk downstairs." He was quite willing to run down if they had asked it, but they didn't; so he walked.

The supper was a typical Southern supper, well cooked, and there was plenty of it. Sadipe addressed himself to the pleasant task of putting himself on the outside of as much of it as a real hungry man who understood his business could, with decency and consistency. After supper he went up to the parlor with Miss Swift and asked her to play something on the piano for him. Like a sensible girl, she sat down to the instrument and played the "Bohemian Girl"[51] with the skill and technique of a veteran performer. Sadipe was charmed, and told her he was immensely pleased, that he was passionately fond of music, and that her playing had almost made him forget his experiences and troubles in coming to this place.

"Do you play, Mr. Okukenu?" she asked, naively.

"Yes," he replied, "though not as well as you, Miss Swift."

"Please let me be the judge of that," answered Miss Swift, leaving her place at the piano. "You will do me a great favor, Mr. Okukenu, if you will be so good as to oblige me with a selection of your own choosing. Here are three or four big books of music, vocal and instrumental."

Sadipe sat at the piano, and picking up one of the books, running through it hastily, his eye fell upon "The Ascription of the Evening Star," from "Tannhauser."[52] Opening the book, he studied it for a moment, and then placing it before him he played the beautiful melody with much expression, bringing out of it a wealth of sweetness and harmony. While he yet played, Principal Swift and Mrs. Swift entered the parlor and sat down near their daughter, and drank in the sweet notes which Sadipe's deft fingers were bringing out of the piano. When he had finished, all unconscious of the presence of Principal and Mrs. Swift, he turned on the piano-stool to ask Miss Swift how she had liked his performance, and then for the first time realized that he had an audience of three instead of one, as he had supposed. All of them were loud in praise of his skill as a pianist. Miss Swift averred that he was a more expert performer than she, and that she was ashamed, since hearing him, that she had played for him first, and thought that he was real mean not to have told her at the beginning that he could play.

The evening passed off pleasantly. Miss Swift recited from one or two of her favorite authors, Dunbar and McGirt;[53] Professor Swift sang very sweetly "Rocked in the Cradle of the Deep"[54] in his fine bass voice, to the accompaniment of his daughter, and Mrs. Swift sang with magnificent effect "Good-by" by Tosti.[55] Sadipe, who possessed a sweet tenor voice, sang an African love song to his own accompaniment, and Miss Swift looked (as she no doubt felt) quite sentimental, and her eyes followed Sadipe during the evening until he said goodnight, and retired to his room for needed rest. But he did not rest, for his mind was uneasy. Before he retired he wrote a letter to General De Mortie, and this is what it contained:

Sadipe's Letter.

——, S.C., 18—.

Dear Sir: I have scarcely been in this place twenty-four hours, but long enough to satisfy me that I shall not be contented or happy here. I do not like the place nor my present environment. I cannot here breathe freely the air of freedom. Where freedom is throttled and manacled it cannot survive, and this seems to be its condition here.

The principal of this little school and his wife and daughter are very agreeable people. The school, as I have gathered from a brief talk with the principal, is just an ordinary school, the promoters of which have a most extraordinary ambition to make it a college. Its curriculum does not begin to compare with that of our little village school in Maine, and I should have no difficulty, were I going to remain, in passing the examination for admission to all its departments in about two days or less. I am disappointed and disgusted, and I have decided to return to Maine so soon as I can communicate with my friends there, and have advised them of the conditions which I find here. I have received a fairly good education in Maine and I thought to be able to get the polish on it here—vain thought. During our conversation on the train you intimated that you had a friend who is establishing an International Detective Bureau, and that you thought you could influence him to employ me. I think now that I should like to engage in this work, and I am vain enough to believe that I have some talent for this kind of work, so if you are of the same mind I would feel very grateful if you will use your good offices with your friend in my behalf, and I trust that before you take any steps in the matter you will communicate with my friends in Maine whose names and addresses I gave you. I am now in captivity, humbled and humiliated, and am therefore the more anxious to break the chains that bind me.

Very truly yours,
Sadipe Okukenu.

The Black Sleuth

Two days after this letter was posted it was received by General De Mortie with a batch of mail which awaited his return from a pleasure trip up the beautiful St. John's River, in Florida, whither he had gone with a party of congenial friends for an outing. He was at breakfast in the magnificent dining-room of the famous Ponce de Leon Hotel[56] when the polite waiter handed him the package of letters and papers which he had forgotten to take after an interesting chat with the clerk at the desk in the main office, on his way to breakfast. He was just on the point of returning for them when the waiter entered the great dining-hall and handed them to him. He glanced over them quickly, and picked out two or three of them, the superscriptions on which were familiar to his eye; these he laid aside to enjoy their contents while he ate. He ran through them again, as if looking for an important letter, and laid aside two others; one of them was Sadipe's; the handwriting was new to him and he scrutinized it critically. The letters of his name were regular and uniform, and the writing showed character and strength of mind. What particularly impressed him was the neatness with which the letter had been addressed. He could not place the correspondent, nor could he wait even to read his good wife's letter before finding out the name of the writer of the letter before him. So, taking up his penknife, he carefully opened the envelope and satisfied his curiosity. The letter was from Sadipe, written in faultless fashion, and very much resembled copperplate; every "t" was crossed and every "i" was dotted, and its whole general appearance was satisfactory and pleasing to the eye of the kind-hearted old general. Laying it aside with a satisfied smile, he opened another, his wife's, read it, made a memorandum on the margin, and placed it in his pocket. The next one he opened was not to be so easily disposed of; it was an autograph letter from a great statesman in Washington, D.C., and like Melchisidek, had neither beginning nor ending.[57] So, at least, thought the general. As he could make neither head nor tail of the wonderful production, he folded it, replaced it in the envelope, and laid it aside. His breakfast was now ready, and pushing his mail to one side he addressed himself to its dispatch with the vigor and energy of a man thoroughly hungry. After breakfasting he gathered up his mail, and taking a toothpick, sauntered leisurely to the waiting-room, where he procured writing material and answered all save one of the batch of letters which he had received that morning. To Sadipe he wrote:

St. A————, Fla.,—18—.

My dear young friend: I am happy to receive your nicely written letter, and to hear from you so soon after my arrival here. I was quite sure after my talk with you on the train that a change of environment would not heighten your opinion of America, at least of this part of it. I did not care to advise you at that time, but now, since you are resolved to leave these parts, I advise you to lose no time in getting away. The South is a veritable hell for a man of your culture and taste, and if you remain here you will either be compelled to swallow your pride by submitting to further indignities, or fight. I am very busy this morning, but I will take the time to write to my friend in your behalf, and will urge him to give you a position. A man of your spirit and talents has no business in the South.

Your friend,

H. B. De Mortie

P.S.—I will see to it that you get the position. H.B.D.

Saturday morning's mail brought Sadipe the general's letter, which he read eagerly and placed in his pocket. Professor Swift came for him about 11 o'clock for a walk through the town, which he had expressed a desire to see. A half hour's walk sufficed. He had seen enough to strengthen his purpose to shake the dust of that town off his feet. White men and even children whom the two had met in their walk stared at him and alluded to him as "a new coon," "buck nigger," "a shade," and other choice terms peculiar to a class of whites in the South. The professor cautioned him to pay no attention to these insults, as if he did there would be trouble. Then it was that Sadipe proposed that they return to the school grounds. He was boiling within, and it seemed that he must speak or burst. But he forebore, survived the ordeal until safely within the school grounds, when he told the professor very frankly what he thought of the town and the people in it, with whom he had come in contact, and expressed surprise that a man of his education and training could so long submit to such brutal and cowardly insults as had been heaped upon them in the few moments they had been thrown in contact with the white people.

"We were better dressed than any white man or boy that we met in our walk," said the professor, "and our prosperous appearance angered them. The poor whites here are lazy and shiftless, and all of them have the idea that they are superior to a Negro, no matter how ignorant they may be. They know that you are a stranger hereabouts, that you are different in manners from the everyday, ordinary Negro they meet, and that accounts for their display of bad manners. I never pay attention to them. I go on and attend to my business and do not notice them any more than if they were not on earth."

"For my own part," said Sadipe, "I would never submit to such indignities as were offered us this morning without making a vigorous protest."

"Which would mean a riot," said the professor. "A black man has not only to swallow his pride, but all the insults the white people choose to heap on him."

"Indeed," said Sadipe, shaking his head, "there are some queer things going on in your country, professor."

The following Saturday Sadipe took part in the exercises in the chapel, and very greatly surprised and astonished the faculty, the students and visitors, and this is how he did it:[58]

(*To be continued.*)

CHAPTER IX

There was the usual hurry and bustle among the students to attend the special missionary meeting in the college chapel, which had been hastily arranged by Professor Swift for Saturday morning, 11 A.M. A returned missionary who had spent many years in Western Africa, Rev. Silas Skinner, of the M.E.[59] Church South, was in the city, and the local pastor had expressed a desire to have him address the students to tell them something of his experiences among their heathen brethren in Africa. The principal was greatly interested in the missionary, the more so since he had among his students a real live African, whom he thought would be glad to hear from home, and so he readily assented to the plans of Dr. Givin to hold this special meeting for their benefit.

Promptly at 10:30 the students began to assemble, and soon filled the benches, which were arranged semicircle that they might all get a focus on the distinguished visitor. The girls occupied the seats on the left, the young men those on the right. After they had all been comfortably seated, the principal, followed by Dr. Skinner, the local pastor of the white Methodist Church, Rev. Mr. Givin, and the assistant principal, stepped from a side door opening upon the platform and took seats. Some of the girls had placed two large vases containing magnolias, wild roses and honeysuckle on the speaker's desk, and the air was fragrant with the odor of these flowers.

At a signal from the principal the College Glee Club took up its position on the platform and sang very sweetly the coronation; at its conclusion the principal offered prayer, after which the assistant principal read the Scripture lesson. The Glee Club sang another selection, and then Dr. Skinner was introduced in fulsome phrase by the principal. Dr. Skinner was well named; he was a tall, lank, gawky specimen of the Southern white man, who in slavery days might have been taken for an overseer or a Negro trader. He had the high cheek bones which distinguish the mountaineers of Kentucky; a heavy-set under-jaw, which indicated bulldog tenacity; steel gray eyes, and a voice like a foghorn. No Southern Negro talked a broader dialect than Rev. Dr. Skinner. He spoke with a drawl, as Southerners who address Negro audiences usually do, and with much looseness of statement and self-confidence.

His talk was of the stereotyped kind. Much was said of the wonderful achievements of the white Christians of America in foreign lands, of the wisdom of God in directing men everywhere to turn their thoughts toward Africa, China, and Japan, and the islands of the sea, by inference intimating that if He had not put it into the hearts of the "all-powerful white race" to stretch hands across the sea and lift up these people they would all be eternally lost. He alluded to the Cimmerian[60] darkness which overshadowed Africa, particularly of the ignorance and superstitions of its peoples, and the great responsibility which their condition placed upon the "favored race," to whom Almighty God had delivered the message and upon whom he imposed the duty of lifting these black heathen, who were degraded and benighted, up to the light of truth. What the white man has done for the Negro in America he can and must do for the Negro in Africa—give him civilization, teach him morality, educate his head, heart, and hand, and thus make him useful to his kind.[61]

He concluded his address by requesting the Glee Club to sing Bishop Heber's hymn, "From Greenland's Icy Mountains,"[62] which it did. Principal[63] Swift opened the discussion which followed, and commended the speaker's zeal and interest as well as the self-sacrificing spirit he had shown in going thousands of miles away from home to teach black men how to find Jesus, to carry the message of good-will and brotherhood to those who sit in darkness.[64] Several of the students spoke expressing a desire to go into the missionary field and do what they could to enlighten and lift up their brothers in Africa when they had finished their education. The principal called upon Sadipe to say a word, and in an aside to Dr. Skinner proudly told him that the young man was a native of Africa. Dr. Skinner looked uneasy, and shifted rather nervously in his seat.

As Sadipe arose to speak their eyes met, and there was fire and several other things in the young African's eyes when he stepped out from the front row of benches and advanced to within two feet of the platform. Looking Dr. Skinner squarely in the eye, he said: "Mr. Chairman," and said it in a clear, ringing voice, which indicated that there was going to be an eruption. Dr. Skinner leaned back in his chair and averted his eyes. Sadipe advanced a few paces further to the front, where he could get a good focus on the missionary, who was now getting uncomfortably red in the face, and continuing his remarks said: "I do not think, Mr. Chairman, that I care to discuss the address delivered by this excellent gentleman; it would take too long, even if I were inclined to do so. Many of his statements about Africa and its people are erroneous and misleading; some of them unworthy of serious thought, but I will say this much: that the so-called 'heathens' of Africa are not nearly so barbarous and inhospitable to the stranger within their gates, nor are they as inhuman and bloodthirsty as the so-called civilized white Christians of the South, who burn Negroes at the stake and hang them from trees and telegraph poles, as I have learned that they do, since my sojourn in this country. The African, heathen or civilized, is hospitable and generous to strangers. Your white Christians whom I have met in this section are most inhospitable and insulting to strangers if their faces, like mine, happen to be black. I am at a loss to understand why the white Christians of America, with all their prejudices to race and color, persist in sending missionaries to Africa and the islands of the sea to civilize and Christianize the 'heathen,' as we are called, when there are so many heathen at their own doors who need the light of the Gospel, and to be taught good manners.[65] But, as I remarked a moment ago, I do not intend to go into the details of this remarkable address. As a loyal and patriotic African it is my duty to say, in all courtesy and kindness, that your speaker's characterization of my people as barbarous and ignorant is not absolutely correct. (Sensation.)

"I wish now to speak briefly of the hymn which we were asked to sing at the close of his remarks, and which I did not join in singing because it is an insult not only to Africans but to Greenlanders and others whom it describes as 'heathens,' whose faces are red, black, brown or yellow—all the so-called weaker races, whose weakness consists in being unlike the Anglo in that they do not covet their neighbors' goods and are not engaged in cruel warfare to extend their power, reaping where they have not sown, and spreading desolation and woe with the battleship, the maxim[66] and other death-dealing instruments. The weakness of these races will prove the sources of their greatest strength when the awakening of nations, which is fast approaching, takes place.[67] No black man who understands the meaning of words can sing this hymn and retain his self-respect. It is written, as you who listen to me may know, by Bishop Heber. It is a hymn written from the Anglo-Saxon standpoint, and it does not conceal the *ego* which inspired it and keeps it alive. It is a hymn imbued with the spirit of boasting. It is written for a race at a time when human slavery dulled the consciences of men. It was not written for all humanity, but for a part of it. It must be quite as absurd for a Greenlander

(*To be continued.*)

CHAPTER X

as for an African to sing it and make melody in their hearts to the Lord. The lips of the Greenlander and the African may sing it, but their hearts and their intelligence would not accept it. It is written for lips that are neither Greenlandine nor African. It was written to stir up the missionary zeal of the Anglo-Saxon. It was not written to infuse inspiration or supply aspiration or zeal to the Negro or Greenlander. While we observe that the license of poetry did not brush away the ice from Greenland's mountains, the natural condition placed there by the Creator of races and humanity, while the spirit of poetry did not fail to discover that dark Africa is a libel, and that only sunshine Africa can produce sunny fountains, and while the natural riches of the country, the 'golden sand,' the 'ancient rivers,' the 'palmy plains' come with a panorama of grace hard to be denied, the offset on the side of man was equally repelling. Africa and India, two great historic peoples, were the objects of song, and the 'spicy breezes' of Ceylon were also carefully conjured up, but can the African or Indian or Greenlander say:

> "'They call us to deliver
> Their land from error's chain.'

"Who calls? Whose land? Thank God that every prospect pleases; but is man really and only vile? Is the Indian, African or Greenlander only vile? Common courtesy would forbid such an aspersion, but race pride is the most irreligious, uncivil and unreasoning thing in the world. We are grateful that the gifts of God are strewn with lavish kindness everywhere in Africa; but is heathenism confined to Africa? If the heathen in his blindness bows down to wood and stone, what do the Anglo-Saxon Roman Catholics do with images and idols in their churches? Would it be wrong to say the Anglo-Saxon Romish Christian, whose 'souls are lighted with wisdom from on high,' in their wisdom 'bow down to wood and stone'?

"The other verses speak for themselves. I have merely called your attention to the libelous and insulting character of this white man's missionary hymn, and hope that it will never again be sung by Negroes in this chapel."

With this parting shot Sadipe sat down, and Dr. Skinner rose up. All eyes were fixed on him, even Professor Swift saw a new light. The shot fired by the young African had gone home, and it hit the mark. The missionary from Africa, his face flushed and his eyes snapping, showed that he felt the keen thrusts of the young student, but he was too diplomatic and too much of a white man to publicly acknowledge that a Negro had worsted him in argument. He coughed up a smile, a sickly, hectic smile, and taking an attitude said:

"It has given me very great pleasure to be with you this morning, and I feel very grateful to your principal for the honor of an invitation to speak to you young Negroes. I was particularly interested in the remarks of the last speaker, who, I am told by your principal, is an African, a native African. He is a very able and logical speaker, and he gives promise of becoming an orator of no mean ability. His remarks were very interesting and very instructive, and I am sure that all of you enjoyed them as much as I did. I hope to have the pleasure of addressing you again at some future time and of hearing this young man speak. I regret that I cannot remain to hear other addresses, because I have another appointment to speak, and I am going to ask your principal to permit me to withdraw, though not before thanking you most heartily for your generous attention." The principal smiled his assent, and, rising, escorted Drs. Skinner and Givin to the street door and gracefully bowed them out. There were only two other brief addresses, but they were pointed and peppery, disclosing the fact that Sadipe had not wrought in vain. The meeting soon adjourned and the students went to their several rooms, or lingered about the campus until dinner time.[68]

The local newspaper, *The Evening Scimitar,* issued an extra about 1:30 or 2 o'clock about the size of a theatre programme, which purported to contain a full report of the meeting and of the several addresses there delivered. Although there had been no representative of the paper present, there was a very fair account of the proceedings, with a left-handed compliment to the Glee Club and some remarks about the natural gifts of the Negro in the direction of music. Then in a double-column, double-leaded[69] article of a quarter of a column, with a big scare head,[70] was given extracts from Sadipe's address, which was followed by an editorial, also double-leaded, the tenor of which was that "higher education is not good for Negroes, as it makes them uppish and impudent to their superiors and raises false hopes in their minds about equality, and also gives them false notions and ideas of their importance. The extracts from an address by a young darkey at the darkey college this morning, which we are publishing in another column of the *Scimitar,* will, we think, open the eyes of the thinking white men of this section to the importance of the fact that the best possible education for the darkey is that comprehended in the three Rs, and not too much of that."

When the *Scimitar* reached the campus numbers of students were there gathered in groups of two and three discussing Sadipe's speech. They were unanimous in the opinion that it was a good speech, and said so among themselves. When they read the *Scimitar* they were more convinced that the speech was all right, because that paper insinuated that it was all wrong. The white people of the town talked about it for days. The principal saw danger ahead for his school, and became convinced after many talks with leading white citizens who had approached him on the subject that the young man ought not to

The Black Sleuth

have been allowed to make such an address. One white man was frank enough to aver that no Negro had a right to call into question any statement made by a white man. But the horse was now out of the stable.

In trying to explain it away to these white people the principal made a mess of it. He could not tell them why he had not asked the young man what he was going to say, and they were not satisfied with his statement that he had not thought it necessary to ask him, since the meeting was not political but religious in character, for an outline of his speech.

He was told that he should have warned this young darkey of the strained relations between the races in the town, and advised him to say nothing that would be likely to give offense to the white people. The idea of a darkey questioning the veracity of a white man! This was a serious offense, and the white people of that community would not tolerate anything of the kind.

The principal was *sore* distressed. Here was trouble all around him and in the distance, and he was not happy by any means. But we will leave him to fight it out his own way.

When Sadipe left the chapel he went direct to the principal's house, where he found a letter and a telegram awaiting him from his friend, General De Mortie. The latter advised him that the position he sought with the International Detective Bureau would be given to him, and that letter followed. The letter told him that he had been appointed special representative of this bureau, that he must leave at once for New York City and meet General De Mortie at the Grand Union Hotel in two days from its receipt, when he would introduce him to the chief of the bureau, who was then on his way from England, and who was scheduled to reach New York on the same day Sadipe was expected to arrive.

A good-sized bank note was enclosed in General De Mortie's letter to Sadipe, with his compliments, with the message that, "Philosophers seldom have any money."

Sadipe said nothing to any one about his good fortune, but he quietly got together his effects and prepared for the journey northward.

As he had only two days to reach New York, he decided to leave the town at midnight on the midnight train. He had heard of the row which his remarks had caused, had read quotations from them in the *Scimitar,* and he realized that if he remained among these people there would be trouble. He chose, therefore, to go.

When the principal came to supper that evening he passed up to Sadipe's room, an unusual thing for him, and found the young man busy packing his grip.

"Why, what's up, young man?" he asked.

"O, nothing special. I am just preparing to return to the North. That is all," answered Sadipe.

Under different circumstances this explanation would have called for a vigorous protest from the principal, but he was too shrewd and crafty a man to offer an objection in this case, and it would not have mattered if he had. The very thing Sadipe was preparing to do voluntarily was the thing which a committee of white citizens had that forenoon[71] urged the principal to compel him to do under penalty of losing the annual State appropriation for his school, some eight hundred or nine hundred dollars, which they assured him would not be forthcoming if this darkey was allowed to remain, and so this cowardly principal had gone to Sadipe's room to break this news gently to him and urge him to leave town.

"So you are really going to leave us, Mr. Okukenu?" he asked, in a tone of mock regret.

"Yes, sir; I am. I could not think of remaining in a place where there is so much of the spirit of the devil and so much unreasoning race prejudice."

"Well," said the principal, "I do not blame you for going, for, as you say, there is a great deal of prejudice, and it is a bad place for a man of spirit like yourself. For you to remain here longer would mean that sooner or later you would be assassinated or lynched by some white tough or by a mob. The white people are aroused over your remarks today in answer to Dr. Skinner. You have stirred them up, and the *Scimitar* is fanning the flames. I don't want you to go, Mr. Okukenu, and yet I do not want you to stay. You are too manly and courageous to be murdered for opinion's sake, and this I am sure will be the sequel of today's meeting if you remain."

"Indeed, is it really as serious as that?" asked Sadipe.

"Yes," answered the principal. "You do not understand these Southern whites as we who were born among them do. We who are indigenous to the soil know them as they know themselves."

Sadipe opened his hand-bag, and taking therefrom the revolver which General De Mortie had given him on the train, examined it carefully and placed it in an outer pocket of his coat. "Professor," said he, "I am leaving this place at midnight. Can you arrange to get my traps to the station in time for the 12:47 train?"

This announcement took the load completely off the principal's mind, and he told Sadipe that he would have one of the students drive him to the station at any hour he wished, and that there was an earlier train that left at 10:32, an express that went right through to Washington, making only one stop.

"Then I will take that train," said Sadipe. "Kindly see that my bags are removed to the lower floor, and that your carriage is ready for my departure at 9:30."

"Young man, I am very sorry you are going from here," said the principal. "Indeed I am, but I cannot conscientiously advise you to remain. You will need some money. Will you accept this bill?"

"Thank you; no," said Sadipe. "I am well supplied with funds, and I could not accept charity."

"Oh, I didn't mean that," said the professor, who saw his mistake. "You misunderstand me. I meant it as loan, assuming, of course, that your finances are at a low ebb."

"I greatly appreciate your kindness," said Sadipe; "but I must even refuse to accept a loan. You know Shakespeare says, 'Neither a borrower nor a lender be.'[72] I have quite enough to carry me to my destination and a little over."

"I am glad to hear that," said the principal. "Well, I will have the carriage ready for you at 9:30. Let us now go to supper." Sadipe put on his collar and followed to the dining-room, where he ate a hearty supper. After supper he went to the parlor and amused himself playing on the piano until the carriage was announced. His bags and boxes were hastily bundled into it, and a big box of lunch was given him by the principal's wife, containing sufficient food for at least four days' journey. He said his good-byes to the household and beamed meaningly full upon the principal's pretty daughter, who proffered her hand just as he was about to step into the old ramshackle family carriage. Grasping the extended hand, he shook it warmly, and said good-bye, and took his place beside the principal, and was driven rapidly to the station, arriving there within fifteen minutes. After attending to the purchase of his ticket and the checking of his baggage, he was ready when the lumbering express train rolled into the station to shake the dust of that town off of his feet and turn his face northward. He bade the young man who drove him to the station a hasty good-bye, at the same time pressing a crisp new $2 bill into his hand as he left the carriage with the principal, who saw him get on the train and who also shook his hand with more than usual warmth, and said good-bye with an unction which concealed more than it revealed.

At 12 o'clock that night the principal stood in his nightrobe at an open parlor window facing an infuriated mob of white men and half-grown boys, and was saying to it: "Gentlemen, upon my word of honor, the man is not here. I expelled him from this school today, and he left town tonight."

"Well, you open thet do', Mr. Nigger," said a coarse white brute in the crowd, "and let us see if thet coon is raley gone as you say."

"Open the do', Nigger," yelled the mob, and the door was opened instanter. But the bird had flown, and the mob retired in disgust. The next and succeeding chapters will tell of the great diamond robbery and the part that Sadipe played in running down the thieves.

(*To be continued.*)

CHAPTER XI[73]

Three years have elapsed since the events herein recorded took place, and Sadipe, our hero, has made his mark in a calling for which nature seems to have specially fitted him.

From the day he entered the service of the International Secret Service Bureau[74] to the hour he rounded up on foreign shore four of the most skillful swindlers on the continent of Europe his career as a sleuth had been an Iliad of successes. He seemed to have been spurred on, inspired by the sneering allusion to himself by Captain De Forrest as "that Nigger" when the superintendent had told the captain he was going to detail him to the case about which they had talked. On that day Sadipe had registered a vow that he would make a record that would compel the narrow-gauged American sea captain to own the force of the Negro's genius and to acknowledge that he is a man.[75]

After Captain De Forrest had purchased the diamond, of which we have already spoken, from Mojola he placed it in his strong box in his cabin, and on his return from South Africa to London he consulted friends who knew much about such things, and on their advice took the stone to the well-known firm of Cheltenham, Sykes & Co., lapidaries and wholesale jewelers to the trade, to be cut and polished. This was one of the most reliable firms in London, and in order that Captain De Forrest might have no difficulty in transacting his business with this firm his friend, Lord Cromartie, gave him a letter of introduction to Mr. Cheltenham, who introduced him to the manager, Mr. Sykes, after they chatted for some moments together in the office. This had the desired effect. Mr. Sykes was all attention and patience.

"I know," said the captain, "absolutely nothing about diamonds, except that they have a way of sparkling in the dark and glittering in the sunlight. Beyond this my experience of their commercial value is as dense as my ignorance of Sanskrit."[76]

After the usual exchanges of commonplaces incident upon the presentation of a letter of introduction from a man of Lord Cromartie's standing and wealth, Mr. Sykes, who was an expert and recognized authority on diamonds, gave the captain the benefit of his large information and knowledge of the commercial value of the product of auriferous[77] earth by subjecting the specimen shown him to every known test to determine its quality, its geological classification and its value. When he had completed his examination he turned to his visitor and said:

"I find this to be a perfectly flawless stone. It looks like a pure white African diamond. As it now stands it is worth a thousand pounds sterling. It is a very rare species of diamond, and when it is cut and polished it will double its value. Sir, I do not believe that there is another like it in all England. May I ask where you obtained it, Captain De Forrest?"

"I bought it from a black fellow in South Africa on my last voyage out there."

"Ah, I see," said Sykes. "I knew it was an African stone. These South African diamonds are the purest in the world and fetch the highest prices. This is certainly the largest one I ever saw."

The captain's eyes sparkled.

They soon got down to business, and the firm was given the order to cut and polish the stone. The captain said that he was going on a voyage to the Indies on the 15th of the month and would probably be absent four months. He would leave the stone and get it on his return to England. Mr. Sykes called in a notary, who drew an agreement which stipulated that in the event of his death, proof of which was to be established to the firm's satisfaction, or failure to call for the diamond at the time agreed upon, or within sixty days thereafter, it was to be delivered to the person named in this agreement upon the payment of all charges specified herein for labor performed and for its safekeeping.

As the captain was a bachelor, he made this agreement—a sort of last will and testament—in favor of a personal friend to whom he was very much attached, and whose name, rumor said, would some day be changed to De Forrest. The agreement was duly executed in duplicate, the captain retaining a copy and paying the notarial fees, to which Mr. Sykes objected unavailingly. He paid also four pounds ten on account, and took a receipt, which, together with the agreement, he placed in his big leather wallet. These details over, Mr. Sykes wrapped the stone in raw cotton, placed it back in the box which contained it, and placed the box in the safe, closed the ponderous doors and turned the combination. Then he gave the captain a receipt for the stone which contained its weight, color, size and general appearance and its approximate value. The captain pulled from his pocket three big cigars and laid them on Mr. Sykes' desk, telling him that he would find them particularly good. Mr. Sykes loved nothing better than a fragrant Havana, and he felt more than compensated for the time and attention he had given the captain by this gift.

After the captain left the office Mr. Sykes took his knife and cut off the end of one of the cigars and lighted it carefully. He smoked it a few seconds and said to himself, "I should say that this is a good cigar, Captain; come again." He unlocked the safe, took out the captain's diamond and stepped across the hall with it to Mr. Cheltenham's office to show it to him. Mr. Cheltenham was the senior member of the firm, very rich, and was dignity personified. When Mr. Sykes opened the office door he saw a visitor, and was in the act of withdrawing, fearing to obtrude.

"Come right in, Mr. Sykes," said Mr. Cheltenham. "I was just about to send for you."

Mr. Sykes entered, and was introduced to the visitor, Colonel Ewart

George Evelyn Bradshawe, K.C.B., R.A.,[78] a gentleman of imposing presence and many medals. The colonel was quite affable, and received the introduction with the quiet dignity and graciousness of manner of the well-bred gentleman, and sat down.

"Colonel Bradshawe has just come to consult us about a stone which he has purchased on 'spec,'" said Mr. Cheltenham.

"Oh, I see," said Mr. Sykes. "Let's take a look at the sparkler, Harry. Have you examined it?"

"No," said Mr. Cheltenham. "I was just on the eve of sending for you when you came in. Here it is. I wish you'd test it. It looks all right, but I am afraid it isn't, as I have said to the Colonel."

"Suppose you gentlemen step into my room," said Mr. Sykes, rising and leading the way. This room was a combination of office and workshop. It contained shelves, bottles of chemicals, queerly constructed scales, and in one corner a quantity of quartz. Near the window [were] a big desk, and two chairs, and a wooden bench. The gentlemen entered and were given seats, and Mr. Sykes proceeded at once to subject the stone to a test. First he weighed it, the result was not satisfactory—a stone of its size should be heavier. Next he took a polished diamond from the safe, which was of the same physical conformation and the same size, and weighed them separately. Colonel Bradshawe's diamond weighed three karats less than the other. Mr. Sykes shook his head. Then he submitted it to another test

(*To be continued.*)

CHAPTER XII

known to diamond experts, and still found it wanting. Whereupon he frankly but delicately informed its owner that the thing was glass.

"What you say, it is glass?" asked the Colonel, eagerly.

"It is nothing else, except that it is a good imitation."

The Colonel affected to be very much put out by the discovery, and said he had been deliberately robbed by the man from whom he purchased the stone. "It is a very fine imitation of a genuine diamond," said Mr. Sykes, "and that is as near as it is to being a diamond. There are great quantities of these on the market now. They come from France, where they are sold by the bushel."

"I purchased it from a French sailor for 10 pounds sterling," said the Colonel, "and I thought I had a bargain."

"No," said Mr. Sykes; "it was the sailor who got the bargain. He was a very lucky man to get so much money for such a cheap piece of glass." And, going to the safe, where he had placed the Captain's uncut diamond when he came from Mr. Cheltenham's room, he took it out and, exposing it to the Colonel's view, said: "here is a diamond worth owning. It is the most perfect uncut stone I have ever handled."

"Oh, by the way, gentlemen, what are your charges for making this test? I beg your pardon for interrupting you, Mr. Sykes," said the Colonel.

"We only charge *for testing diamonds*, Colonel, and since this is glass, there will be no charge," said Mr. Sykes, in his politest tones. Reverting again to the Captain's diamond, he produced a stone about the size of an English walnut, which he said had just been left by a gentleman to be cut and polished, and which in its present state was worth at least a thousand pounds if it was worth a penny.

"Whew!" exclaimed Mr. Cheltenham.

"Good gracious!" chimed in the Colonel. "It must be a fine one!"

"It is," said Mr. Sykes, holding it up between his thumb and forefinger. "It is a pure white South African stone. I have examined it carefully, and there isn't a flaw in it. This greatly enhances its value. It is one of the largest clear white stones I have ever seen. When polished it will be one of the most valuable stones in the United Kingdom. I do not believe its equal will be found for years to come in all the world."

"Pray who is the Croesus[79] to whom this valuable and priceless gem belongs?" asked Colonel Bradshawe innocently. And before he could think Mr. Sykes had given the name of the owner of the stone.

"Indeed!" said the Colonel. "I know the Captain well. I met him at one of the receptions of the Governor General in India some three years ago. Fine old fellow he; deucedly clever and rich beyond the dreams of avarice. Well he can afford diamonds of that size."

Mr. Sykes felt some relief when he learned that the Colonel and the Captain knew each other, and for the moment thought no more of his bad break in revealing the name of a patron to a comparative stranger. Mr. Cheltenham and the Colonel then had a look at the stone, examined it closely, noted its weight and decided that it was just what Mr. Sykes said it was—a rare and valuable stone. Then Mr. Sykes took it, placed it in its bed of raw cotton in the box from which he had taken it, and, putting it carefully into the safe, closed the door and turned the combination.

The Colonel's visit was cut short by the entrance of other callers on business and after returning his thanks to Messrs. Cheltenham and Sykes for courtesies shown him, he bade them good-morning with an unctuousness which Mr. Sykes, who knew a few things about human nature, noted and remembered.

The Black Sleuth

When Colonel Bradshawe got outside the great establishment he collected his wits and did some thinking. One of the important things he did was to inscribe in his notebook the name of the owner of the diamond he had been permitted to see. His next move was to locate Captain De Forrest, to ascertain the name and whereabouts of his ship, whither she was going, if she had not already sailed, and when she would return to this port. He walked rapidly, and was soon at the door of his humble lodgings, entering which he found his confederates awaiting him, to whom he gave a detailed account of his morning's work and his failure to dispose of his "spurious diamond." One of the party was a beautiful English girl with sparkling black eyes and lips that were the color of a ripe Delaware peach that has been kissed by the sun. To her he said: "You must find this Captain De Forrest." She understood and in less than an hour she was on his trail.

It was Machiavelli who said: "Men are so simple and yield so much to necessity that he who will deceive will always find him that will lend himself to be deceived."[80]

With consummate judgment, Colonel Bradshawe laid his plans, and thus far they had been worked out with a cleverness and skill which had been as brilliant and successful in execution as they were bright in conception.[81]

His male chum and confederate, Algernon Hodder, was directed to locate the captain's ship. This was an easy task, since all vessels that entered port are required to register, giving name of master and owner, where from, character of cargo, etc. So Hodder went out next morning, and was absent just two hours by the clock. When he returned he brought this memorandum: "'The Norris K. Peters,'[82] Captain Geo. De Forrest, master, American merchant vessel, trading in East Indies, sails September 15 on six months' voyage; captain boards at Royal Arms, is rich, fond of good wine, pretty women and curios." Hodder passed the "memo" to Colonel Bradshawe, who read it aloud, remarking that he commended the captain's good taste in preferring the company of pretty women and for liking good wine. This was a great combination, "by Jove." Whereat all the party joined in a hearty laugh, and before the echoes of it had died away Miss Crenshawe, who had been sent on a similar mission to that of Hodder, entered the room and reported progress. She had located The Royal Arms, and had found out several other useful things. Colonel Bradshawe then called them all around him and laid before them his plans to entrap De Forrest, which was as follows: Miss Crenshawe was to be sent to The Royal Arms daily for luncheon, and in the most aristocratic turnout to be found in London. She was quietly to learn all she could about the captain, his habits, etc., and, if possible, to get up a flirtation with him. This plan was at once decided on as the first step, and was to go into operation the next day.

Now, The Royal Arms was one of the new fashionable hotels of London that employed a black waiter, in compliment to its American patrons, who made it their habitat during the London season, and Sadipe, our hero, who was not ignorant of the plot which had been hatched to rob Captain De Forrest, had communicated to his chief his desire to be placed in this menial position. Accordingly a representative of the bureau called on the proprietor of The Royal Arms, and, after explaining the object of his call, asked that Sadipe be thus employed. The request was immediately granted, and on the following day Sadipe was installed as a waiter. He knew as much of waiting as a boy, but he was quick to learn, and he did learn several of the little tricks of the profession, and in about a week was as obsequious a dining-room genuflector as could be found in all London.

On the day that Sadipe took service at the Royal Arms Miss Crenshawe made her appearance at the noonday luncheon of this fashionable hotel. She arrived at the hostelry on the hour, in a handsome equipage, with liveried coachman and footman. When the vehicle stopped in front of the ladies' entrance to The Royal Arms there stepped from it a gorgeously attired lady in silks and laces and glittering jewels, whose presence attracted the attention of the habitues. [She also wore a][83] hat, which set off her beautiful face to advantage, and there was something of the patrician in her queenly bearing. She walked with dignity and grace to the door, at which stood a liveried servant, who threw it wide open as she entered, bowing with the grace of a courtier as she passed by on her way to the dining-hall.

Her cheeks were the color of June roses, and under the soft yellow light of the huge electroliers,[84] in the hall leading to the dining-room, she was a picture of loveliness. Her eyes sparkled as she strode to the table assigned to her. Guests who were returning to or going to lunch could not resist the temptation to cast furtive glances at the beautiful creature. One male guest who had already lunched and was leaving the hall returned and, taking a seat at a table near that which she occupied, ordered another lunch and ate it slowly.

The Negro waiter, being something of a novelty in England, and particularly in The Royal Arms, was much in demand by the guests. We will call him Randolph, because that was not his name. When Miss Crenshawe had been comfortably seated she beamed on Randolph sweetly, and the man who had followed her into the dining-hall looked daggers at the black man. Randolph, who was standing in front of her table with folded arms, awaiting her pleasure, advanced at a nod from her and, bending sufficiently low to catch her softly spoken words, learned that she wished for her luncheon two French chops, rolls, a cup of coffee and—"Yes, that will be all at present." Randolph attended to this order promptly, and while he was away Captain De Forrest entered the room and went to the table which he usually occupied, and which was diagonally opposite that of Miss Crenshawe. He did not at first observe the fair creature. He was busy with the shipping column of the *Thunderer*. He laid the paper down for a moment to make a memorandum, and his eyes wandered and fell upon the bewitching beauty opposite him. Picking up his paper again, he held it so that he could see over the top of it without, as he thought, being observed. Presently his eye fell upon another man at a side table, who was intently gazing in the same direction as himself, and who found time to bestow a scowl on him. The lady was, or acted as though she was, unmindful of what was going on in a quiet way.

She did not once look in the direction of either of her unknown admirers, and when Randolph returned with her luncheon she laid a shining silver coin beside her plate for him, and asked him in her soft, sweet voice to fetch her a pitcher of ice water. Randolph procured a pitcher, filled it with cracked ice, and filled the lady's glass as deftly as a veteran waiter could have done. "Take this; it is yours," she said, pushing the coin toward him. Randolph took it and, thanking her with a pretty little bow, he withdrew to a respectable distance. Presently she raised her arched eyebrows and smiled sweetly. Randolph advanced toward her: "Waiter, can you tell me the name of that fat gentleman sitting opposite my table? He has been staring at me ever since he entered the room. Is he the proprietor?"

"O, no, miss, that gentleman is a wealthy old sea captain. His name is De Forrest, and he owns a ship called the 'Norris K. Peters.' He is a bachelor, and stays in this hotel the year around when he is not on a voyage." This was all said in a low tone of voice.

"Thank you," she said, bestowing another of her bewitching smiles on the black man, and then she ordered another chop and a glass of milk.

While Randolph was gone Miss Crenshawe, who was something of an artist, took from her handbag a visiting card and pencil, and made a clever outline sketch of Captain De Forrest, who had tired of gazing upon her lovely features, and was now strenuously introducing a beefsteak with the concomitants into his interior.

When Randolph returned Miss Crenshawe finished her luncheon, paid her bill, and swept out of the dining-hall as majestically as she entered it. Her carriage awaited her, and she stepped into it and was driven to her apartments.

As soon as she had left the room both Captain De Forrest and the strange man plied Randolph with questions about her. Who is she? What is her name? Where does she live? He did not know—that is, he told them so. But he had photographed her face in his memory, and no matter what her disguise in future, he would know her. He had seen her before, and he was sure that he would see her again.

(*To be continued.*)

CHAPTER XIII

Hodder's coup in locating the "Norris K. Peters," finding out when she was to leave port, her destination and the habits of her master, was no less a brilliant piece a work for a tyro than was Miss Crenshawe's triumph in bearding the lion in his den and taking his picture. She had succeeded admirably in attracting to herself the attention which she craved of the giddy old man who was later to become as tractable as a kitten under her hypnotic influence. And we must not forget Randolph, the black, whose role in this little drama, about to be enacted, was, to say the least, as difficult as it was delicate and dangerous, yet for which he was admirably fitted in view of the fact that his black face disarmed all suspicion as to his true character. To this precious quartette full of complacent conceit of their specie, he was simply a blackie. So far as they knew he was simply a few removes from a benighted heathen, and, unlike the Anglo-Saxon, incapable of understanding the meaning of things said in his presence. He was quiet, unobtrusive, obsequious, a model servant. Hodder, who had lived in South Africa, where Englishmen whose education is defective spell Negro with two "gs," was wont to remark when speaking of Randolph to his companions: "he's a well-set-up nigger, and he's deucedly polite, don't you know. I really like him." Before Randolph was detailed to the Royal Arms, the manager of the bureau had called him into consultation, and discussed with him the details of this case, and he reminded him that since he was so versatile and resourceful, it remained for him to make a record as a sleuth, and run down the thieves who had stolen the diamond which Captain De Forrest doubted the ability of a nigger to recover.[85]

"There are several persons under suspicion, Mr. Okukenu," said the manager, "but this bureau has been unable to find a clue. It has run down at least ten of the cleverest crooks in England, and it is satisfied that they knew practically nothing about the robbery of Captain De Forrest. So that we are now convinced by certain developments of recent occurrence that it was the work of an organized band of thieves who knew what they were about and have skillfully covered up their tracks."

"I see," said Randolph. "I called at the Royal Arms yesterday to see a friend of my father—an Englishman who has lived many years in Africa, and while we sat in his room talking, a card was brought to him by a messenger. He read the name aloud, and told the boy to send the person up. When the visitor entered the room, I perceived that he was some officer of high rank, for he wore many medals and was particularly well groomed.

"'Colonel Bradshawe, I believe,' said my friend, rising and offering his hand, which the colonel took, shaking it warmly

"'Yes, that is my name, sir,' he replied.

"'Be seated, sir,' said my friend. The colonel took an armchair. 'I am very glad to meet you, Colonel Bradshawe,' continued my friend. 'May I ask the purpose of your visit, sir? I do not recall that we have ever met before.'

"'Why, don't you remember me, Mr. Stoughton?' asked the colonel, with a trifle too much anxiety in the question.

"'You certainly have the advantage of me, sir. Will you be good enough to tell me when and where we have met before?'

"'Why, certainly. I was introduced to you above five years ago at a reception at the Governor-General's in Calcutta, where my regiment was at that time stationed.'

"'By whom, please.'

The Black Sleuth

"'By the Governor-General himself,' said the colonel, coolly.

"'Ah, yes, yes, I quite well remember you now. There was a lady with you. As I recall the circumstance, a very attractive, a very beautiful lady, colonel. By Jove! I shall never forget her face. Was she your wife or a relative, colonel?'

"'She was my w-i-f-e.'

"'Ah, yes. I remember now she was introduced as Mrs. Bradshawe. Pardon my stupidity.'

"'Why, certainly, Mr. Stoughton. One can not be expected to keep all the details of these social functions in one's head.'

"'Quite right, my dear colonel.'

"And changing the subject, Mr. Stoughton asked the colonel what brought him to London at this season, and when he would return to Calcutta.

"'Oh, I had some leave coming to me, and I concluded that it would not be a bad idea to spend as much of it as I could among my kindred and friends in dear old England.'

"'Is your lady with you, colonel?' asked Mr. Stoughton, innocently.

"And Colonel Bradshawe evidently forgetting that he had given his 'lady' the place of honor in a former answer about her, unwittingly answered that his friend, Miss Crenshawe, would remain in Calcutta for some time yet.

"Mr. Stoughton looked at Sadipe,[86] who was an interested listener, and at Colonel Bradshawe, who never realized he made a decidedly bad break, and he looked the confusion which he evidently felt. Mr. Stoughton repeated the name Crenshawe several times, and Colonel Bradshawe's color came and went. That he had made a tactical blunder was clear enough by referring to his 'lady-wife,' if she was really his wife, as Miss Crenshawe. It put that person in the attitude of a mistress, and it did not speak well for the morals of either the colonel or his lady. Mr. Stoughton recalled that some years ago there had been printed in the *Calcutta Times* a salacious story about a young woman of the name of Crenshawe who had only recently come out from England and in some mysterious manner had ingratiated herself in the confidence of a rich old man who had made an immense fortune in Kimberley, South Africa. Such was her influence over him that he allowed her to pass as his daughter. Finally there was a scandal, followed by the discovery that the old man had been robbed of thousands of pounds and a lot of valuable jewelry, many pieces being heirlooms which had been in his family since the reign of Henry VIII.[87]

"'I wonder,' asked Mr. Stoughton, 'if this young woman is related to the Miss Crenshawe of whom I have spoken?'

"Colonel Bradshawe's face took on a deep crimson hue. He coughed and fidgeted about in the big armchair for a second or two before he answered. He said:

"'Really, Mr. Stoughton, I could not say as to that; but I do not believe that this young woman is related to the one to whom you allude. I think I remember that circumstance. The woman was captured by Scotland Yard men, and before she could be locked up she took poison and died a violent death within two blocks of Scotland Yard. Well, I must be leaving now, Mr. Stoughton. I heard you were here, and I merely called to pay my respects and to renew old acquaintance,' said Colonel Bradshawe, rising, hat in hand, and moving toward the door.

"'Must you really go so soon, colonel?' asked Mr. Stoughton. 'I fear I have bored you. Here we have been talking for almost an hour, and I haven't given you an opportunity to say a word. Bless my soul, they do say that we old men are garrulous; that when we get wound up we cannot stop. Ha! ha! ha!'

"And Mr. Stoughton arose and extended his hand to the colonel, who bowed himself out as graciously as he knew how. Sadipe, who had been sitting by a window reading a copy of the *London Mail*, found time between periods to observe certain things which struck him as being worthy of more than passing notice.

"'Did you ever meet this colonel before, Mr. Stoughton?' asked Sadipe, with a twinkle in his eye.

"'Well, I was just thinking about him as you spoke, Mr. Okukenu. I have an indistinct recollection of having met a colonel out in India with a name sounding very like this, but he was a much stouter and larger man than this Colonel Bradshawe. I am not sure that I have ever met him socially, but I did not wish to embarrass him by telling him that I did not know him. I presume he is some adventurer with a scheme.

"'I did not like his answer about his wife or lady,' said Sadipe. 'A married man never alludes to his wife by her maiden name when speaking of her to others.'

"'True,' said Mr. Stoughton. 'I noticed that myself, and I am the more convinced that the man is a fraud.'

"'Have you a copy of the *Army Gazette?*' asked Sadipe.

"'Yes, there is one there on the shelf to the right, Mr. Okukenu,' replied Mr. Stoughton.

"Sadipe reached for the ponderous tome and requested to be shown the card of the colonel. Then he turned down two pages of the big book carefully, but he found no such name as Bradshawe and no such regiment as that given on his card in India or anywhere else.

"'This is remarkable, Mr. Stoughton,' said Sadipe. "I do not find the gentleman's name in the *Gazette.*'

"'No?' answered Mr. Stoughton.

"'No,' said Sadipe, 'it is not here.'

"'Well, I should say it is remarkable,' was the brief answer of Mr. Stoughton.

"And then the conversation drifted to the West Coast. Sadipe asked about his old father and friends of his boyhood days, and his old teacher, who had gone out to England and returned to the West Coast. Mr. Stoughton gave him full particulars of the most important events which had transpired since he came away from his fatherland to tempt fortune in the Western Hemisphere. They chatted over these things for more than an hour, and then Sadipe took leave of his father's old friend, promising to call again at the first convenient opportunity."

On his way to his lodgings he thought of Colonel Bradshawe, and the more he thought of him the more he was convinced that he was a counterfeit. Instead of going directly to his room, as he had intended, he called a cab and directed the cabby to drive him to the International Bureau, where he found the manager up to his neck in work.

"Mr. Hunter," said Sadipe, "I have a clue to the De Forrest robbery."

Mr. Hunter looked up from the batch of papers he held in his hand and, gazing at Sadipe, asked: "What makes you think so?"

"I have met today a Colonel Bradshawe, a very voluble gentleman, who claims to have served in India."

"Bradshawe! Bradshawe!" repeated Mr. Hunter. Describe him, Mr. Okukenu."

"I will," said Sadipe. "A man of medium height, florid complexion, about forty years of age, auburn hair, and eyes almost blue; talks rapidly, and does not look you in the eye when speaking, and is rather reserved in manner."

(*To be continued.*)

CHAPTER XIV

Mr. Hunter pulled out a drawer in his desk, and taking therefrom a package, opened it, and selected a photograph from the package, which he handed to Sadipe, and asked him if the man he had seen in Mr. Stoughton's rooms looked anything like the man whose picture he saw before him.

"Why, Mr. Hunter," said Sadipe, "this is the man I met in Mr. Stoughton's rooms today; the very man, sir! How do you happen to have his picture here? Is he a crook, a burglar?"

"Yes, he is both a crook and a burglar, and one of the most expert cracksmen[88] in the three kingdoms,[89] Mr. Okukenu. There isn't a more polished or gentlemanly swindler and confidence man in all England."

"Gracious," said Sadipe. "He must be the dean of the profession; and where has this distinguished and accomplished specialist been keeping himself that you have not been able to mingle with him in social alliance, Mr. Hunter? You know you somehow manage to meet all the social lions that come to London, and I am a little surprised that this gentleman has escaped your argus[90] eyes."

Mr. Hunter made no reply to this criticism beyond laughing heartily at Sadipe's keen thrusts.

"You are sure, Mr. Okukenu, that this is the man you saw today (taking the photo from him)?"

"Mr. Hunter," said Sadipe, "an African, and I am told that a North American Indian, never forget a face they have once seen. Have you ever met this man Bradshawe, Mr. Hunter?"

"Oh yes; I have seen him several times."

"Very good," said Sadipe; "then let me make the identification more complete, for I fear you are disposed to doubt its accuracy. This man whom I met today has dark-gray eyes, walks with a shuffling gait, talks with great deliberation and never looks you in the eye when conversing with you. There is on his right cheek a small mole, and behind his left ear a small patch of gray hair, probably a birthmark, for he is much too young to be turning gray; he can not be much over five and thirty."

"Your supplementary description tallies exactly. You have certainly seen the man we have been looking for for so long a time. I am thoroughly convinced that the man you have seen and describe is the man we want, and that he is not, as we have been led to believe, in France, but is, as the journalists say, 'in our midst.'

"Now, since you have discovered him, Mr. Okukenu, I am going to detail you to effect his capture, and this office will give you all the assistance in its power to enable you to bring about his capture. You ought, of course, to know something about this fellow, so that you may go about your work intelligently. In the first place, his name is not Bradshawe; that is one of his many aliases; his real name is Algernon Mandeville, and he is best known at Scotland Yard and by all our profession as 93,008. His photograph representing him in many disguises may be seen in the police headquarters of nearly all the capitals of Europe. He is one of the smoothest, slipperiest rascals that ever cracked a safe or picked a pocket, and he has done both and escaped punishment, for no one has yet been able to fasten either of these crimes upon him. He is said to be the dishonored son of a nobleman, who himself figured in a court scandal many years ago and retired to his country estates to live it down if possible. The boy was splendidly educated, and graduated with honors for the bar, but after his father's downfall he went to the bad and began a life of riotous living in which wine and women played their usual parts, with the result that young Mandeville was tabooed by his former friends, and so turned 'gentleman burglar.' He is a fine linguist, speaking French, Spanish, Italian and German with fluency and correctness. He has been a bogus French count, Spanish don, Italian prince and a German Baron, and has mingled in splendid alliance with the best blood of Europe without discovering his real identity for months after he has played his part, leaving behind him a trail of bad debts and unsavory stories. I was present at a social gathering in Vienna[91] in the summer of 1899[92] at which he was a guest, though I did not then know who he was, and I have only come to know him since by his photographs, nearly all of which I have seen. When the main topic of conversation was about a disgraceful scandal in Genoa in which a certain French Count Gevé De Alvord figured with the wife of a foreign minister who was spending the summer there, and who lost her jewel bag and a large sum of money after a carriage ride in the suburbs with the count, who mysteriously left town the following day, the lady, for prudential reasons, could not afford to make much noise about her loss, heavy as it was, but the facts leaked out some months after she had gone. She was an American lady, and you know American ladies are fond of titles, real or bogus. 'Count De Alvord' appears to be a man of discrimination and tact, and to have been very successful among these lion hunters. I saw him on the occasion of which I speak listening intently to the recital of this incident in his career, and at its conclusion he smiled one of those cynical smiles which are indulged in only by those who are sure of themselves. I can never forget the expression on his face when Baron Felderstrum, a Swedish nobleman, asked, 'Who is this Count De Alvord? I never heard of him before.' Mandeville has excellent control of himself. Beyond coloring slightly he betrayed no other symptoms of alarm or fear. Taking from his pocket a large silk handkerchief, daintily perfumed, he remarked to the lady who sat next him, 'It is oppressively warm here, madame. Let us get nearer a window.' And suiting the action to the word he arose and taking the lady's arm, escorted her to the farther end of the spacious salon, to a window which overlooked a garden filled with choicest exotics. He was in another atmosphere. So, you see, my dear Mr. Okukenu, with whom you will have to deal."

"Yes," replied Sadipe, "and yet I believe I shall be able to run down this man, clever as he is."

"Very good, very good," said Mr. Hunter. "Tomorrow you shall have a trial of your skill as a sleuth. If you round up Mandeville, your reputation as a thief catcher will be made, and you will be able to command the largest fees paid to the profession in the United Kingdom."

"Tomorrow didst thou say, Horatio?"[93] said Sadipe, with a merry twinkle in his eye. "I will make the preliminary trial tonight. I will locate this versatile and thrifty gentleman, and will thereafter camp on his trail until he is safely landed behind the bars."

"Good! Good!" said Mr. Hunter. "I have every confidence in your ability and in your judgment. You Africans have many advantages over us Europeans, and there are some things which you can do better than we when you try. Your black face will be an important aid in the capture of Mandeville (if you capture him), and your knowledge of French will come in handy, for in the presence of strangers he always converses in that language, and he will never suspect that you understand that tongue."

Sadipe smiled, and rising, bade Mr. Hunter good night.

Our hero went forth from the presence of his chief with a fixed determination to locate "Colonel Bradshawe," and ultimately capture him. The insulting words of Captain De Forrest, "You don't mean to say that you are going to turn this case over to that nigger," still rung in his ears, and he renewed his vow to make the Yankee captain acknowledge the force of his genius as a sleuth, not only by capturing the thief who had stolen the diamond which he had lost, but by recovering the diamond itself.

In four hours after leaving Mr. Hunter's office Sadipe, disguised as an African student, of which at that time there were many in London, pursuing their studies in the law and medicine, strolled into one of the many music halls of the great metropolis to enjoy the singing, and incidently to get a little refreshment. Sitting down at a table in the rear of the great hall, a pretty English barmaid hastened to him to learn his wishes. He ordered some crackers and a mug of ale, which he sipped slowly, occasionally munching a cracker to kill the bitter taste of the ale, of which he was not overfond, but which he drank on the advice of his physician, more as a strength-giving tonic than as a beverage. He had gotten into the hall just before the orchestra began its part of the elaborate program arranged for the evening. The only song he heard (and he was particularly fond of vocal music) was De Lara's beautiful song, "The Garden of Sleep," which was admirably rendered by a buxom English lassie with wonderfully red cheeks (suspiciously red) and a voice of remarkable volume and purity, which penetrated every corner of the great hall. When the last note died out, the audience rose to its feet and applauded the singer so vociferously that she responded with an *encore*, Lassen's "All Souls' Day," which evoked as much applause as the former song. Sadipe ordered another mug of ale, and started the applause afresh, and kept at it so industriously and energetically that the now overworked soloist gave "Within a Mile of Edinboro Town." The audience was enraptured, thrilled, charmed, delighted, and clamored for yet another song from the fair singer. But the manager, as soon as she had finished this song, quickly advanced to the front of the platform and announced that the orchestral concert would now begin, and read from a slip, which he held in his hand, the numbers which it would play. Among them were included: "Hoch Hapsburg," J. N. Kral; "Dans Tes Yeux," E. Waldtenfelt; Waltz, "Bleue," Margis; March, "Crusader," Sousa; "Queen of the North," Bucallassi; "Irish Patrol," Puerner; March, "Punjaub," G. Payne; Waltz, "Greek Slave," S. Jones; Finale, "God, Save the King."[94]

Each number was well executed. The orchestra was composed of Englishmen, East Indians, Africans, and one Russian. The audience, a large one, representing many races and classes of society, enjoyed this part of the program immensely, judging from the manner each number was received and applauded by it. Even Sadipe joined in the general acclaim. When "God, Save the King" was played the audience rose to its feet, and part of it sang the words of this particular air. Standing in a front seat in the first gallery, near the stage, was "Colonel Bradshawe" in military uniform, and a few of his many medals, a vizorless cap in his hand, and the inevitable monocle.[95] Sadipe got a glimpse of him, then a full view, then a quarter view.

"I have him," he said to himself; "no matter how he dresses or disguises himself, I can never forget that face. Where I see it I will know it."

When the orchestra ceased playing, the audience passed out. Sadipe, whose seat was near the door, sat down until the crowd thinned out, and passed out just as those from the upper floors were going out. As "Colonel Bradshawe" came down the stairs Sadipe stood a little to the side of the main entrance, where he could get a full view of him. As the "Colonel" stepped in the street Sadipe fell in with the passing throng, and shadowed the "Colonel" for six or seven squares. He turned into a side street, just off the main street, and walked rapidly to the red brick house midway of the block, and giving a sharp whistle, waited a moment or two, when the street door was opened by a woman who greeted him with a merry laugh, and he entered quickly, after tossing into the street the butt of a Havana. Sadipe crossed the street and took the number of the house, and walking rapidly to the corner, hailed a passing cab, which he heard approaching, entered it and directed the cabby to drive him to his lodgings. The following morning bright and early he was on the trail of the "Colonel." At exactly 8:25 he saw the "Colonel," accompanied by a woman, descend the steps of this house and pass up the street to the corner, where there was a cabstand. After a few words with the driver they both got in and were driven away. Sadipe took a cabriolet and directed the driver to follow the hansom cab, which had just left the stand. The first cab was driven at a smart pace to the Royal Arms Hotel, about twenty squares away. The second, in which sat Sadipe, which was only three or four minutes behind it, stopped there also. Sadipe gave the driver half a crown, told him to wait, and went in. Approaching the clerk's desk, which commanded a view of the spacious dining-room, he inquired what the rates were for breakfast, and ordered that breakfast be served him at 10:30.

As he walked slowly to the street door he saw through the huge plate glass window which separated the rotunda from the dining-hall, "Colonel Bradshawe" and the lady who accompanied him from the house we have mentioned at breakfast. Jumping into the cab, he directed the driver to take him quickly to the office of Mr. Hunter, and in less than a quarter of an hour he was seated in the private office of his chief, to whom he gave a detailed statement of all that he had accomplished the night previous; and on that morning Mr. Hunter was pleased with the progress he had made and told him that he was doing finely.

"You had better send a messenger back to the hotel, Mr. Okukenu, with a note cancelling your order for breakfast," said Mr. Hunter; "and as it may be in the course of preparation I will just give you a small check to cover its cost. It would not be fair to order it and not pay for it, even though you do not eat it. Now that we are certain about the identity of our man, we must devise some plan to get him without creating a scene. What do you suggest, Mr. Okukenu?" asked Mr. Hunter.

"Well," said Sadipe, "if I can get into that hotel as a waiter, I may be able to get evidence enough to convict the 'Colonel' and his confederates, for he has confederates."

"Capital idea," said Mr. Hunter. "I think I can arrange that; but you will have to take off that moustache you wear and those good clothes, and your rings; they can be put in the safe here until this matter is pulled off. I will go right down to the Royal Arms and see the proprietor, whom I know very well, and induce him to take you on as a waiter."

Mr. Hunter then called a messenger boy, a man of about thirty, and dispatched him with the note cancelling the order for breakfast for Sadipe and a check for five shillings. Putting on his hat, he took Sadipe with him to a less pretentious hostelry around the corner from the office, where they had a sumptuous breakfast of fried soles, broiled ham, coffee, boiled eggs, toast and cocoa.

(*To be continued.*)

CHAPTER XV

After breakfast they parted, to meet again at 12 o'clock, sharp. Sadipe went to a barber's and had his moustache removed, and from there to his lodgings, where he donned a cheap black suit with a short coat, such as are affected by hotel waiters, and promptly on the hour was back in headquarters, ready for orders.

Our readers have already been told of the dinner at the Royal Arms, at which Miss Crenshawe contrived to secure an introduction to Captain De Forrest, master of the "Norris K. Peters."[96] "Colonel" Bradshawe, who was an habitue of this famous hostelry, had also cunningly managed to scrape up an acquaintance with the doughty old sea captain. It came about this way: One morning after breakfast he strolled leisurely into the smoking-room, where the captain, with other guests of the hotel, was enjoying his morning paper and cigar. The captain, who was fond of comfort, was seated in the largest and most comfortable armchair in the room. On a small table within reach were several letters which he had opened to read. On the floor beside his chair were the London morning papers. The captain was reading the ship news in the Times and noting with a blue pencil such items as interested him. "Colonel" Bradshawe walked over to where he sat and addressed him as follows:

"My lord, I am delighted to meet you here this charming morning. I have not seen you since we met in India. I hope you are very well."

Captain De Forrest flushed a deep crimson, and, looking up from his paper into the face of his visitor, beheld a fine specimen of manhood in the person of Bradshawe, who wore a military coat, on the left breast of which depended three gorgeous medals. In his right eye he wore a monocle. The captain was flattered. To be taken for a lord of the realm tickled him immensely, and he blushed a deeper crimson as the wily Bradshawe fawned on him. Laying the Times down on the rug beside his chair, he arose and said:

"My dear sir, you have evidently made a mistake. I am Captain De Forrest, of the 'Norris K. Peters,' trading in the East Indies."

"Wonderful resemblance," remarked "Colonel" Bradshawe, the while chuckling to himself at the ease with which the Yankee captain had swallowed the bait. "I sincerely beg your pardon, sir. I was sure you were my old and valued friend Lord Cromartie, of Aberdeen. You look enough like him to be his twin brother. I never saw two men who more closely resembled each other," said the "Colonel," coyly.

The captain blushed again, and looked confused.

"I know Lord Cromartie very well, sir," said he. "We have been friends for more than thirty years, and I am proud of the friendship of such a man."

"You speak very well, sir," replied the "colonel." "Lord Cromartie is a most excellent man, and one whose friendship is really worth having. I myself have known him for twenty years."

"Won't you be seated, sir," said the captain, drawing a chair for the "colonel."

"Thank you, yes," answered the "colonel," sweetly, as he seated himself in the armchair opposite the captain.

"And now, my dear sir," said the captain, "we have had a most delightful chat about a mutual friend. Be good enough, if you please, to inform me whom I have the honor of addressing. Your face is familiar, though I do not recall that we have ever met socially."

The "colonel" apologized for not having disclosed his identity earlier, and producing a beautiful Russia leather card case he extracted therefrom one of his visiting cards, containing his name, all his titles, and a coat of arms.

Adjusting his glasses and reading the name, Captain De Forrest extended his hand to the "colonel," who grasped it and smiled a self-satisfied smile.

The captain asked the "colonel" if he smoked, and being answered in the affirmative handed him his cigar case, from which he took one of the big black Havanas, such as the captain always smoked, and which the "colonel" lighted. Soon the two men were energetically puffing away at the fragrant weeds and filling their section of the smoking-room with smoke.

For nearly an hour the two talked, smoked and swapped stories. The "colonel" was greatly pleased with himself in that, without any apparent effort, he had been able to obtain from the captain information which would be useful to his clever female accomplice, who had already begun her campaign, with a fair chance of winning.

One of the results of this chance (?) meeting between the "colonel" and the captain was a dinner given in the honor of the captain and a few friends by "Colonel" Bradshawe in one of the handsome private dining-rooms of the Royal a week after their first meeting.

At the dinner at the Royal Arms "Colonel" George Evelyn Bradshawe renewed the acquaintance with Captain De Forrest, and introduced the "old salt" in effusive phrase to the "beauty" whom to know he had been willing to pay Sadipe a handsome fee. Of course, the captain was inexpressibly happy. His joy was unbounded, and his vocabulary contained no word which could adequately express the great pleasure it gave him to meet such a charming and attractive personality as Miss Crenshawe confessedly was. It is amusing to watch an old man when [he] is in love with a pretty face, to note his grimaces, to listen to his silly and vapid inanities, and it is equally amusing to see with what ease and skill a young and experienced adventuress, who understands her business, can twist one of these silly old fools around her finger and bend him to her will.

Captain De Forrest had yearned long and earnestly for the opportunity which was now his. He was basking in the smiles of one of the cleverest adventuresses in all England. He was loath to leave London, no, not that, he was loath to leave behind him the soulful eyes, the cherry red lips and the bewitching smiles of the woman who had ravished his silly old heart without his exchanging a dozen words with her. Of course he did not know that this was her specialty, and she did not tell him.

There is a vulgar phrase to the effect that "there is a sucker born every sixty seconds."[97] Captain De Forrest was one of the early species, and he had swallowed bait, hook and sinker. Miss Crenshawe had him completely in her power, and if she told him to stand on his head, old as he was, he would have attempted it.

The quartet, after dinner at the Royal Arms, and the good-byes had been said, held a conference to determine upon the plan of attack when the captain should return from his contemplated trip to the East Indies. It was decided, since he was so completely "gone" on Miss Crenshawe, to give him a return dinner this time. Miss Crenshawe was to be the hostess, and the guest of honor was to sit at the same table with her where he could feast his eyes on her beauty to his heart's content. The beauty, in the meantime, was to lead him gently on and find out things about the wonderful diamond, its value, its location, and what use was to be made of it. All this was agreed upon without demur, for it had been made clear to all who had observed the captain's actions during the dinner that day that he was an easy mark for Miss Crenshawe, and that she, better than any of the company, could handle him according to her own sweet will. The quartet, having agreed to this much, decided to have a luncheon in the Royal Arms the following day, to formally ratify their action with wine and song and a few general remarks.

Promptly at 2:30 the next day they met, as per agreement, but in another section of the great hotel, in one of the private dining-rooms, and Sadipe, our hero, was detailed by arrangement to serve them. The conversation was in French. English was spoken only to the black. While they were enjoying their luncheon they talked volubly in French of their plans to inveigle the old sea captain into their meshes, and to get possession of the diamond which he possessed. Miss Crenshawe was to make love to him as ardently as she knew how (and she knew how), was to arrange to go with him to the lapidary's where he had left it to be cut, and to do her best to induce him to bring it away with him to show it to "Colonel" Bradshawe, Hodder, and his lady friend, who were consumed with desire to see such a valuable and priceless gem. This accomplished, the captain was to be asked to drink to the health of Miss Crenshawe in a bumper of Mumm's Extra Dry, properly drugged, and at the psychological moment, when the drug had taken effect, [she was] to relieve him of the treasure. The "colonel," his old friend (?), with the assistance of Hodder and the black, were to take the captain for a little air in the carriage, leave him in a room in a notorious resort which they knew, where he would sleep off the effects of the drug, and wake up the next morning in a strange part of London some five or six miles from his hotel. The conspirators were to assemble again at midnight, in tourists' attire, and take a late train for Paris, and on the following day depart for Belgium as quietly and mysteriously as they had entered Paris, where they would take a steamer bound for the United States. Sadipe understood every word they said, and as soon as they had left the room, which they did shortly, after tipping him liberally, took his notebook from his pocket and made several important entries.

As soon as he had cleared the table and put the room to rights he wrote out in detail the salient points of the remarkable plot which he had heard outlined, and communicated the same to his chief.

At noon the following day he received these instructions: "Keep a sharp eye on all these people; report their movements daily—where they go, and what they say; if possible, find the private house where they congregate, and don't let them escape you.   Hunter."

The next day, dressed as a native African, and carrying a grass bag filled with curios from his native land, he made a visit to a house in a side street not more than twenty squares from the Royal Arms. He did not know who lived there.[98] He had passed it many times, and the thing that struck him about it was that, though it was inhabited, the windows and curtains were always down, except those in the English basement, where the servants worked. He knocked on the iron gate, and a sprightly red-cheeked English lassie, with large blue eyes, laughing eyes, opened it, and instantly remembered him from having seen him passing at other times. She knew or believed that he was a peddler, and asked him what he had to sell. Sadipe dropped into pidgin English, and said:

"Me show you, lady, many beautiful tings made in my country. I sell 'em cheap. Yo want buy some ting today?"

"Oh, I don't know," said the girl. "Come in and let me have a look at your trinkets." And she opened the gate wide and passed the black into the servants' reception-room, where there were several chairs, a big round table, on which were a few copies of old magazines and newspapers and a pack of playing cards.

Sadipe advanced toward the table and, opening his bag, put a number of articles on view. Among them were some curiously wrought work baskets made of the tough African grass, and highly colored, and some really pretty floor mats made of the same material.

While the two maids were examining these Sadipe picked up the playing cards and began to shuffle them. One of the girls, noticing him, asked him if he could tell fortunes.

"Oh, li'l bit. W'y yo wan' fortune tole?" he asked.

"How much?" asked the girl.

"Me tell yo lots for shilling," answered Sadipe.

So a bargain was struck immediately, and the other maid, who had been listening to the conversation, withdrew, closing the hall door, and left the black man and her fellow-servant together.

Sadipe proved to be so clever with the cards that the girl looked at him in amazement. He told her her name, age, and the details of a love affair of her earlier life in which the only man she had ever really and truly loved had been accidentally shot on the morning of the day they were to be married. That she was now engaged to a man whom she had only recently begun to doubt, that her doubts were well founded, as he was already married. He described the man so accurately that the girl gave a faint scream. Recovering from her excitement, she told him to "Go on, go on."

"No more," said Sadipe. "It is not good fo' yo' know too much."

She paid him the shilling and called her friend into the room and held a whispered conversation with her, the result being that Sadipe had to tell her fortune also.

"Can you read palms?" she asked Sadipe.

"Yes, me tell fortune wid card, wattah, and read face."

"I want you to read my palm."

Sadipe took her slender hand in his and scrutinized closely the lines below the "mount of Venus."[99] The first words uttered were:

"Yo' have a long life an' yo' marry rich man, but he not in dis country. Yo have trouble much. Dere is one woman who love dat man same like yo', but he no love her." (The girl shuddered.) "He true to yo'. She try pizen him when she no make him love her, an' she goin' write yo' one bad letter, try scare yo', but yo' must not notice dat. Yo' lover he by yo' side in sixty day. Yo' catch one letter from him inside tree day, an yo' will be very happy woman."

The girl smiled, and Sadipe went on reading her palm.

(*To be continued.*)

CHAPTER XVI

"He bring you beautiful presents, much gold and fine goods. He is make rich where he bin, and you will go back to de lan' where he come from. He is tall man wid black hair and big heart and he love you same as he love his life."

The description of the girl's affianced was perfect. She was delighted with the reading and cheerfully yielded up the shilling charged.

Both the girls then made a number of purchases, and just as Sadipe was about to go the beauty of the quartet, of whom we have been talking, came into the room to give some orders and, espying the black, recognized him as a peddler from whom she had some time ago purchased some curios, and asked what he had new and to show her his stock.

"He tells fortunes beautiful," said one of the maids in the tone of voice of a person who had gotten a quid pro quo for value received.

"Oh, he does, eh?" replied her mistress. "Has he told yours?"

"Yes'm; an' he's told it true—told me things that nobody except the Lord, my sweetheart and myself could know. That he did, ma'am."

"Well," said madame, "he must be a real genius. I will have to test his wonderful powers as a seer. What are your charges, my good man, for lifting the veil and giving us a peep into the future?"

Sadipe shook his head, as though not fully comprehending this flow of language, and was silent. Milady, seeing that her words were lost, said:

"I want my fortune told before I buy anything from you. How much I pay you?"

Sadipe's eyes brightened at the prospect of another customer, and he replied softly:

"Me charge one shilling, lady."

"Very well. How do you tell fortunes, by cards or the palms?"

"Any way you like me to do, lady," said Sadipe.

"Tell it by the cards," she said, drawing a chair up to the table on which Sadipe had spread his wares. He began to shuffle the cards vigorously, and while he was doing so both the maids retired from the room and closed the door between, leaving their mistress and the black alone. When he had finished shuffling the cards, he asked her to cut them in three parts. She did so. He picked up the first part she had laid down, looked the cards over carefully, did the same to the two other parts and then, taking up again the first part, he said:

"There is one very old man who is thinking much of you, but you have not known him very long. He is very rich, has a great many jewels and diamonds and much money. He would marry you."[100]

Picking up the next part: "He is now on the water. He is a seagoing man, and he is now going to a far country. The cargo that he will bring back with him will be worth a king's ransom, it will be so valuable."

Picking up the third part and running them slowly, he said: "He has a valuable gem. It looks like a diamond. It is not with him. It is here in London. You are to get this gem, but he will not give it to you."

Madam looked at the black. He went on:

"There are three other persons besides you who know of this stone, but you only will handle it. You will have it in your hands within sixty days. You have talked with three other people about it within the past forty-eight hours. Its possession will create trouble and bloodshed. You will see this old man and eat with him in less than two months. He will propose marriage to you. You do not love him, though he loves you. You love a soldier. He is a tall man, a great rover and adventurer. The cards say that he will be engaged in a transaction which will involve him and three others in great trouble and probable imprisonment."

Sadipe shuffled the cards again and requested the woman cut them. She did not move nor utter a sound, but sat in her chair, her face as white as a sheet, staring at him. Finally she found her voice and said: "Tell me no more. I have heard enough. Here is your money," and she handed him a half-crown. "Keep it," she said. Recovering from her agitation, she purchased a few trinkets, paid for them and left the room.

Sadipe packed his bag and prepared to follow suit when one of the maids came in, flushed and agitated, saying:

"You told my mistress bad news, didn't you?"

"I told her the truth," said Sadipe, "and I could have told her more, but she would not stay to listen."

"She feels very bad over whatever it was you told her, and she is sitting in the dining-room crying as if to break her heart."

"She will cry harder than that if she does not abandon the purpose of which I told her."

The maid's curiosity was now aroused, and she, with all a woman's artfulness, began to ply Sadipe with questions, promising secrecy if he would tell her what it was he told her mistress which had wrought such a change in her.

"No; that would not be honorable," said Sadipe. "You have no more right to know what I told her than she has to know what I told you. She gave me her confidence as you did, and I am bound in honor not to reveal her secrets or yours."

The maid looked sheepish and took another tack.

"You must have said something to her about the old sea captain who has gone away. I've heard her and the colonel discussing him for hours."

"Colonel who?" asked Sadipe, innocently.

"Colonel Bradshawe," answered the girl.

"Does Colonel Bradshawe live in this house?" he asked the girl.

"Why, certainly he does," she said.

"What does he do? What is his occupation?" asked Sadipe.

"He doesn't do anything," said the girl.

"Who else lives here?"

"There is a new couple here since Monday—a Mr. Hodder and a young woman who speaks French."

Does this Mr. Hodder speak French, too?"

"Oh, yes, they all speak it."

"Do you speak it?"

"Yes, but very imperfectly. I understand it very well. I was a maid in a French family at Bologne—Sur Mer—for five years, and learned to speak and write the language, but I'm a little rusty now."

"Oh, I see," said Sadipe. "Does your mistress know that you speak and understand French?"

"Oh, no," said the girl.

"Very good," said Sadipe. "How long have you lived with these people?"

"Oh, about three years; just three years lacking six weeks."

"Have they always lived in this house?"

"Yes, since I have been employed by them. They sometimes go away to France or Belgium and remain for six or seven weeks."

"Does anybody come here to see them in their absence?"

"Yes, last year they left rather hurriedly at night without saying where they were going, and two or three days after they had gone two men came here looking for Colonel Bradshawe."

"What sort of looking men were they?"

"One was a thick-set man with a heavy beard and a very red face, the other was a tall, slim man with a moustache. The big man was dressed in tweed and the slim man wore a blue serge suit. They looked like business men."

"Did they say what they wanted with the colonel?"

"No; they merely inquired if he was in town."

"Did you give them his out-of-town address?"

"I did not."

"Why?"

"Because my instructions were to give no one his out-of-town address. I simply told them that I did not know what it was."

"But you did know?"

"Yes."

"Well, I must be going," said Sadipe; "but I am coming here again in a few days and will give you a good palm reading, and if you can really keep a secret I will tell you something that will be of the greatest interest and profit to you. You need not say that I have asked you these questions. I will be here in three days, and I shall want to talk with you on a very particular matter."

"Very well, sir," said the maid. "You may trust me. Come when you will."

"Thank you," said Sadipe.

(*To be continued.*)

CHAPTER XVII[101]

On leaving this house, where he had gathered so much valuable and useful information, Sadipe went at once to headquarters, where he reported progress, and to ask for further instructions. He related all the facts minutely to his chief and was complimented by him on his skill as a seer.

Sadipe laughed heartily at the compliment, and said that he did not know one card from another, and that he had merely guessed at the things he told the girls which had pleased them so much and their mistress, to whom his message had given such evident pain.

"So these gentlemen are now out of the city, eh!" said the manager of the bureau.[102] "I thought as much," he added, "and I think I know where they are to be found," he continued. "Your instructions, Mr. Okukenu, are to take the midnight train tonight and go at once to Paris. This time you must travel as a gentleman of leisure, a rich African merchant. This letter will give you full instructions what to do when you reach Paris. You are the only man who can successfully carry out those instructions, and I have implicit confidence in your ability to do so because you have already shown marked skill as a sleuth in that you successfully located the rendezvous of these shrewd swindlers, who have thus far eluded the vigilance of the best detectives of Scotland Yard. Now, if you can see that servant girl again before you go, it would not be a bad idea to question her sharply and find out where

Colonel Bradshawe is, as this knowledge would save time and enable you to go directly to the town in which he is now domiciled outside of Paris."

"But you wish me to go away tonight, and there is no time to see this girl," said Sadipe, "unless my trip can be deferred for, say, two days at most. The girl does know a great deal that would be useful to the bureau, and I believe that if I could see her again and read her palm, as I have promised to do, and would like to do, I could induce her to talk freely, and we could act then more quickly than we will be able to do by my going to Paris and shadowing these people for, say, a week or ten days. She understands French, as she told me, and it follows that she heard this quartette discuss their plans. All we want is the right *clue*, is it not so, chief?"

"By jove!" answered the manager, "your plan is the correct one, Mr. Okukenu. Wait here a few moments until I go into the main office and talk it over."

Sadipe picked up a copy of The Times, which was lying on the manager's desk, and taking an armchair near the window, sat down and was busy scanning its newsy columns. His quick eye fell on an item dated from Rouen, reading as follows:

"Rouen, France, Sept. 19.—At a reception given at the residence of Monsieur and Mlle. Jean Jacques Magloire on Thursday evening last the guests of honor were two wealthy English gentlemen, General Sir Edward Bradford, K.C.B., the Hon. Mr. Hoddersford, and his excellency Count Rudolph Blatzheim, a member of one of the oldest families in Prussia."

The item went on to relate how these gentlemen were the lions of the hour, and how the ladies raved over them, etc., etc.

Presently the manager returned, smiling, and said, "Mr. Okukenu, we have delayed your trip until the day after tomorrow. You will leave at midnight, going direct to Paris, and you will carry out the instructions contained in the letter given you. You are to understand, of course, Mr. Okukenu, that instructions are given to you merely for your guidance and are not arbitrary; that they contain certain facts impossible for you to get except through the bureau's agents in France. You are to use your own best judgment as to methods, and work up this case according to your own plans."

"Very good, very good," said Sadipe, "I understand perfectly."

Picking up The Times, which he had laid on the manager's desk, he pointed out to him the news item which he had read, and asked him to read it, first asking him if he had seen it. He had not, and began to read it with considerable interest. When he finished reading it he remarked, "That is an important piece of news, Mr. Okukenu."

"I should say it is," was all that Sadipe would say.

"I shall be leaving now, chief," he said. "Tomorrow I read palms; good day."

"Good day, Mr. Okukenu."

The following day about 11 o'clock Sadipe, who had donned his African costume, took up his grain bag of curios and wended his way to the house where he had made a reputation as a seer. He found the maids in cheerful mood and glad to see him. They invited him into the servants' sitting room, which had been tidied up, and he took an armchair and began to explain to them why he had called again, so early after his last visit. He said he was thinking of returning to his own country in a very few days, as the climate of England was much too severe to one who had always lived in a tropical country, and as the winter was coming on and as it promised to be a severe one, he would very probably go to Liverpool in the next few days and take ship for his beloved West Coast. He had called to make good his promises to the ladies to read their palms and to dispose of as many more of his African curios as they might wish to purchase of him. The young women said they were very sorry to learn that he was leaving England and they hoped he might return soon.

"I shall be very likely to return," he said; "I like your country very much, and I have met some very excellent people here. England is a great country and English people, when you know them well, are very kind and sympathetic."

Having thus prepared the way and disarmed them of suspicion as to the real object of his call, he said he was ready, if they were, to tell them their fortunes. The cook[103] wanted hers told first, so the house girl went to the kitchen, closing the sitting-room door after her.

"I will make no charge to you for this reading. You have been kind enough to buy my trinkets and I appreciate it very much."

"Oh, thank you," said the cook, blushing; "that is very nice of you, indeed."

"Do you wish me to read the cards or your palm?" asked Sadipe.

"I think I will have you read the cards," she answered.

"Have you cards here?" asked Sadipe.

"Yes," she replied; "in that table drawer there is a new package."

"Good!" said Sadipe, opening the drawer at her direction. He took out the cards and, removing them from the case, began to shuffle them like a veteran soothsayer. The girl drew her chair up to the table and Sadipe passed the cards to her and asked her to cut them in three equal parts. With a great deal of seriousness the girl complied with his request. Sadipe picked up the first part of the three sections, ran them over once or twice before saying a word to her, shook his head, smiled meaningly, and said:

"My young lady, it is better to be born lucky than rich." Laying down a card on the table—the ace of diamonds—he continued: "there is on its way to you a letter from a distant land which contains the best news you have ever received. Following this letter will come to you a sum of money, which you have been expecting for years but feared you would never get, and you will be rich the remainder of your days."

The girl gasped and attempted to speak.

"Wait a moment," he said; "there is some sad news here for you," laying down the ten of spades, "but it is not serious. A relative whom you have never met—an old man who was very rich—is dead. He was some relation to your mother. I see a woman here," he said, showing her the queen of hearts, "who"—

The girl could wait no longer and burst out with the information that the dead man pictured in the cards was her uncle Algernon who had gone out to Australia before she was born, to engage in sheep raising.

95

Then she wept a little, but soon recovered her composure. Sadipe took up the next section.

"You have had a proposal of marriage within the past nine days from a man who knows what I have just told you. He is a messenger in the office of the lawyers from where you will get the letter telling you of your good fortune. If you are wise you will have nothing to do with this man, who is merely a fortune hunter and doesn't love you."

"Oh!" she said, "that is Martin Coverdale."

The king of spades happened to be the next card Sadipe picked up, so he took a chance and guessed what sort of chap Martin looked like. "He is a tall, dark featured man, with very black hair, and dresses well."

"That's Martin," said the girl, and with that Sadipe threw down the king of spades, where she could see it. The girl gazed at it intently for a moment and said, "I'll never marry him."

Taking up the last section, Sadipe said: "Good hearts follow you," throwing down the ten of hearts, "the man who loves you most is the one you think of least, but he is an honest, true-hearted man, and if you marry him will make you a good husband. He is neither poor nor rich, but he has enough to make you comfortable. You met him in a gathering not long ago and shunned him. See," he said, "there's the room" (throwing down the four of clubs) "and there are the people" (throwing down the ten of clubs). The girl was dumfounded, and began to confirm Sadipe's guess.

"That man is Barney Huddleston," she said, "and as true as you live we met at a party the other night, and I avoided him. And you say he loves me?"

"As surely as you live, miss, and better than any man you know. He worships you."

The girl's face beamed with smiles. Sadipe shuffled the cards twice more and told her the same story each time and she was *happy* ever afterwards.

Then she bought a great quantity of his trinkets and gave him 25 shillings as a present for the good news he had brought her.

The Black Sleuth

CHAPTER XVII [Continued]
[104]

"This is all I can now tell you, Miss," said Sadipe. Placing the cards in their case, he opened the table drawer and put them into it.

"You were saying when we last talked together, Miss, that you understood the French language but could not speak it very well."

"Yes, I perfectly understand that tongue, and can speak it; my only difficulty (and it is only the result of carelessness) is that I do not pronounce my words exactly as a French person would, and am sometimes misunderstood because I put the accents in the wrong places."

"Oh I see," said Sadipe, "that isn't a very serious misfortune. You were telling me that your employers often conversed in that language; are they not English?"

"As English as I am," said the girl, "and I was born in Devonshire."

"Well I can not understand why they would speak in French, being English, as you say they are, unless they have something to say which they are afraid to have their servants hear if spoken in English. You are sure that they do not know that you are familiar with that tongue?"

"Quite sure, sir, for I have never told any one that."

"Good, good," said Sadipe. "By the way where have Col. Bradshawe and his friends, Mr. Hodder and the Count, gone? I learned yesterday that they are in France; do you know what town or city they have gone to?"

"Yes, sir; he did not tell me himself, but I heard him in conversa-

97

tion with the Count and Mr. Hodder, say in French, that 'we are going to Rouen.'"

"Did you say Rouen, Miss?"

"Yes, Rouen," she answered.

"Did they say that they were going anywhere else beside Rouen?"

"The Colonel said they would spend four or five weeks in Rouen and then go to Belgium."

"Ah, I see. How long have they been away?"

"Just twelve days."[105]

"Do you know these people very well, Miss?"

"Why, how do you mean?"

"I mean do you know what kind of people they are, whether they are respectable folks or not?"

"Really I see very little of them, especially the men, for they are very seldom here when in England. They go out a great deal in the nighttime and come in very early in the morning and are never seen by the servants except at meals. Sometimes the young woman goes away in a carriage with them and remains out very late."

"You have never seen the old Sea Captain De Forrest, have you?"

"Only once, sir; he was here once before he sailed; there was no one here except Miss Crenshawe and the servants, and he did not remain over twenty minutes. When Col. Bradshawe came she told him in French, while at dinner, that the diamond was safe, that the captain had called while he was absent, to assure her that the lapidaries had about finished cutting and polishing it and that he would surely let her see it as soon as he received it; they both laughed very heartily, though I confess I didn't quite see the point."

"You promised me, Miss, when I was first here that if I confided a secret to you you would keep it; can I trust you with that secret now?"

"I pledge you on the honor of a woman and in the fear of God that I will not divulge to any one the confidence you repose in me, sir."

"I accept the pledge, Miss, in all good faith and will trust to your honor to keep it."

"You may well do that, sir," she answered.

"These people with whom you are living," said Sadipe, "are not honest; they are crooks. Thieves, that is a better word. They are being hunted for many robberies committed by them at various times, but of which there is no direct proof. The men are gentlemen thieves, the woman is an adventuress and is used by these men to inveigle rich old men, and get them into compromising positions, where they fear exposure and disgrace, and force them to pay large sums for immunity. Some day the whole household including the servants will be arrested by the police and exposed."

"Mercy!" cried the girl.

"This is the secret I impart to you, Miss; keep it inviolate. Take my advice and get out of here as soon as possible or your whole life will be ruined."

This ruse had its effect on the girl, who had been considerably wrought up. She regarded Sadipe as a man of mystery since he had revealed to her certain hidden things in her life and she felt that he was able to penetrate her innermost thoughts.

(*To be continued.*)[106]

APPENDIX A

Chapter VII

After eighteen months' hard and conscientious study under the tutelage of Mrs. Pelham, he had exhausted her stock of knowledge, absorbed and assimilated all that she had been able to teach him, and he was now ready for college. Mrs. Pelham had been in her younger days a teacher in a boys' academy near Boston, and she frankly confessed that this black boy was one of the quickest and best scholars she had ever taught. She constantly marveled at the keenness of his intellect, the quickness of his perceptions and the ease with which he grasped and analyzed some of the hardest and most difficult studies she gave him. So that through her his fame went abroad and he became a local celebrity.

At the beginning of the fall term of Eckington College for Negro Youths he found himself the possessor of a scholarship, the joint gift of Mrs. Pelham, his patron, and Colonel Amos Otis, president of the local bank at Sago. The latter was greatly interested in him, as was Mrs. Pelham, and showed him many kindnesses from time to time.

In a few days he was ready for the long journey south. Friends and neighbors of Mrs. Pelham made him little presents of things useful to a young man at school, together with a substantial sum of money, which he at first hesitated to accept, but which he afterward, on the persuasion of Mrs. Pelham, did accept to avoid giving offense to the donors. He was provided with letters of introduction to prominent colored men living in the vicinity of the school, and to a couple of teacher friends of Mrs. Pelham who were living in the town.

On Saturday morning of that week he took leave of his kind patron and the friends who had gathered in the little parlor to say good-bye and to wish him Godspeed and a safe journey, and set his face toward Eckington College, in a far Southern State, traveling as a first-class passenger until he reached the capital city of the nation, which is sandwiched between two of the old slave States, Maryland and Virginia, and where prejudice against Negroes is almost thick enough to cut with a knife. Here, in the home of the President, the seat of power, where the laws which are supposed to govern this nation are made, where equality of citizenship is proclaimed by blatant demagogues in both branches of Congress, where there are more Negroes of all shades and condition than he had ever before seen during his brief residence in America, he received the first great shock of the many which he was to experience during the two days' journey before him.

His train being late in arriving at Washington, his journey was delayed some hours, and he strolled out of the Pennsylvania Station at Sixth and B Streets to Pennsylvania Avenue and meandered leisurely toward the great white-domed Capitol, upon whose highest point the Goddess of Liberty stood in mock seriousness, keeping guard (?) over the liberties and rights of the people. He asked a colored man whom he met the name of the big building and the meaning [of] the mammoth statue. Being told, he jotted down the information in a notebook which he carried. Continuing his journey, he was soon at the Peace Monument, at First Street and Penn Avenue. Here he read and noted in his book the inscription on the tablet at its base, gazed in admiration at the work of the artist, and then, retracing his steps, soon found himself at the starting point, entering the station just as the guard was crying "All aboard! This way to trains for the South!" He started for the gate and attempted to pass through, but the gateman, a gruff, coarse Irishman, stopped him with "Whure is yure ticket, old

The Black Sleuth

man?" Sadipe gave him a look of withering scorn and stepped out of the line. Going over to a window, he searched his pockets for the ticket, which he had securely placed in an envelope with the cash given him by Mrs. Pelham and her friends. Carefully replacing the envelope in an inner pocket with a large safety pin to make sure of it staying there, he returned to the gate and presented it to the ticket man, who scanned it critically before punching it and, slapping Sadipe on the back with his big, red hand, said: "There's yure train, old man. Step lively!"

"You are an insolent, impudent brute! How dare you touch me?" said Sadipe, boiling with rage at the coarse, vulgar utterance and action of the uniformed underling. "I have a good notion to slap your face," said the plucky black boy.

A gentleman who had witnessed the conduct of the gateman and heard his insulting remarks to Sadipe here came forward and said:

"Young man, this fellow has insulted you grossly, and you should report him at once to the company. If you will give me your name, I will myself do so and state what I saw him do to and say to you. I am a stockholder in the company, and am sure the management require that all its employees shall at least be civil to its patrons."

While Sadipe and his new-made friend were talking the Southern train drew out from the station and left him. The gentleman looked at his timetable and told him that there would be another train at 12:37. Going to the telegraph office in the station, Sadipe wired the president of Eckington College that he had missed his train and would leave at the last-named hour, 12:37.

The strange gentleman and Sadipe then sought the office of the superintendent upstairs, where they jointly complained of the conduct of the man at the gate. A messenger was dispatched to bring that worthy to the superintendent's office, where he was confronted by Sadipe and his newfound friend, who recited what he had said and done. The superintendent administered a severe reprimand and warned him that if another such complaint was lodged against him his name would be changed from Mike to Dennis. He suspended him for two days, with loss of pay. Having come off victor in shock number one, Sadipe was introduced to shock number two exactly at 1:25. He was now on the train bound for the South, which was moving quite rapidly and nearing the Virginia line, when the conductor approached and with a supercilious scowl took up his ticket. "Here," he said gruffly; "you belong in the kyar for Nigros. This heah kyar is for white folks only. You must git out'n heah, old man. Yo' kyar is the last but one in the rear. Step lively, now!"

Sadipe could not believe his senses. He was nonplussed, stupefied, and he was also angry.

APPENDIX B

Chapter XVII

"This is all I can now tell you, Miss," said Sadipe. Placing the cards in their case, he opened the table drawer and put them into it.

"You were saying when we last talked together, Miss, that you understood the French language but could not speak it very well."

"Yes, I perfectly understand that tongue, and can speak it; my only difficulty (and it is only the result of carelessness) is that I do not pronounce my words exactly as a French person would, and am sometimes misunderstood because I put the accents in the wrong places."

"Oh I see," said Sadipe, "that isn't a very serious misfortune. You were telling me that your employers often conversed in that language; are they not English?"

"As English as I am," said the girl, "and I was born in Devonshire."

"Well I can not understand why they would speak in French, being English, as you say they are, unless they have something to say which they are afraid to have their servants hear if spoken in English. You are sure that they do not know that you are familiar with that tongue?"

"Quite sure, sir, for I have never told any one that."

"Good, good," said Sadipe. "By the way where have Col. Bradshawe and his friends, Mr. Hodder and the Count, gone? I learned yesterday that they are in France; do you know what town or city they have gone to?"

"Yes, sir; he did not tell me himself, but I heard him in conversation with the Count and Mr. Hodder, say in French, that 'we are going to Rouen.'"

"Did you say Rouen, Miss?"

"Yes, Rouen," she answered.

"Did they say that they were going anywhere else beside Rouen?"

"The Colonel said they would spend four or five weeks in Rouen and then go to Belgium."

"Ah, I see. How long have they been away?"

"Just twelve days."

"Do you know these people very well, Miss?"

"Why, how do you mean?"

"I mean do you know what kind of people they are, whether they are respectable folks or not?"

"Really I see very little of them, especially the men, for they are very seldom here when in England. They go out a great deal in the nighttime and come in very early in the morning and are never seen by the servants except at meals. Sometimes the young woman goes away in a carriage with them and remains out very late."

"You have never seen the old Sea Captain De Forrest, have you?"

"Only once, sir; he was here once before he sailed; there was no one here except Miss Crenshawe and the servants, and he did not remain over twenty minutes. When Col. Bradshawe came she told him in French, while at dinner, that the diamond was safe, that the captain had called while he was absent, to assure her that the lapidaries had about finished cutting and polishing it and that he would surely let her see it as soon as he received it; they both laughed very heartily, though I confess I didn't quite see the point."

"You promised me, Miss, when I was first here that if I confided a secret to you you would keep it; can I trust you with that secret now?"

"I pledge you on the honor of a woman and in the fear of God that I will not divulge to any one the confidence you repose in me, sir."

"I accept the pledge, Miss, in all good faith and will trust to your honor to keep it."

"You may well do that, sir," she answered.

"These people with whom you are living," said Sadipe, "are not honest; they are crooks. Thieves, that is a better word. They are being hunted for many robberies committed by them at various times, but of which there is no direct proof. The men are gentlemen thieves, the woman is an adventuress and is used by these men to inveigle rich old men, and get them into compromising positions, where they fear exposure and disgrace, and force them to pay large sums for immunity. Some day the whole household including the servants will be arrested by the police and exposed."

"Mercy!" cried the girl.

"This is the secret I impart to you, Miss; keep it inviolate. Take my advice and get out of here as soon as possible or your whole life will be ruined."

This ruse had its effect on the girl, who had been considerably wrought up. She regarded Sadipe as a man of mystery since he had revealed to her certain hidden things in her life and she felt that he was able to penetrate her innermost thoughts.

(*To be continued.*)

Chapter XVII [Continued]

On leaving this house, where he had gathered so much valuable and useful information, Sadipe went at once to headquarters, where he reported progress, and to ask for further instructions. He related all the facts minutely to his chief and was complimented by him on his skill as a seer.

Sadipe laughed heartily at the compliment, and said that he did not know one card from another, and that he had merely guessed at the things he told the girls which had pleased them so much and their mistress, to whom his message had given such evident pain.

"So these gentlemen are now out of the city, eh!" said the manager of the bureau. "I thought as much," he added, "and I think I know where they are to be found," he continued. "Your instructions, Mr. Okukenu, are to take the midnight train tonight and go at once to Paris. This time you must travel as a gentleman of leisure, a rich African merchant. This letter will give you full instructions what to do when you reach Paris. You are the only man who can successfully carry out those instructions, and I have implicit confidence in your ability to do so because you have already shown marked skill as a sleuth in that you successfully located the rendezvous of these shrewd swindlers, who have thus far eluded the vigilance of the best detectives of Scotland Yard. Now, if you can see that servant girl again before you go, it would not be a bad idea to question her sharply and find out where Colonel Bradshawe is, as this knowledge would save time and enable you to go directly to the town in which he is now domiciled outside of Paris."

"But you wish me to go away tonight, and there is no time to see this girl," said Sadipe, "unless my trip can be deferred for, say, two days at most. The girl does know a great deal that would be useful to the bureau, and I believe that if I could see her again and read her palm, as I have promised to do, and would like to do, I could induce her to talk freely, and we could act then more quickly than we will be able to do by my going to Paris and shadowing these people for, say, a week or ten days. She understands French, as she told me, and it follows that she heard this quartette discuss their plans. All we want is the right *clue*, is it not so, chief?"

"By jove!" answered the manager, "your plan is the correct one, Mr. Okukenu. Wait here a few moments until I go into the main office and talk it over."

Sadipe picked up a copy of The Times, which was lying on the manager's desk, and taking an armchair near the window, sat down and was busy scanning its newsy columns. His quick eye fell on an item dated from Rouen, reading as follows:

"Rouen, France, Sept. 19.—At a reception given at the residence of Monsieur and Mlle. Jean Jacques Magloire on Thursday evening last the guests of honor were two wealthy English gentlemen, General Sir Edward Bradford, K.C.B., the Hon. Mr. Hoddersford, and his excellency Count Rudolph Blatzheim, a member of one of the oldest families in Prussia."

The item went on to relate how these gentlemen were the lions of the hour, and how the ladies raved over them, etc., etc.

Presently the manager returned, smiling, and said, "Mr. Okukenu, we have delayed your trip until the day after tomorrow. You will leave at midnight, going direct to Paris, and you will carry out the instructions contained in the letter given you. You are to understand, of course, Mr. Okukenu, that instructions are given to you merely for your guidance and are not arbitrary; that they contain certain facts impossible for you to get except through the bureau's agents in France. You are to use your own best judgment as to methods, and work up this case according to your own plans."

"Very good, very good," said Sadipe, "I understand perfectly."

Picking up The Times, which he had laid on the manager's desk, he pointed out to him the news item which he had read, and asked him to read it, first asking him if he had seen it. He had not, and began to read it with considerable interest. When he finished reading it he remarked, "That is an important piece of news, Mr. Okukenu."

"I should say it is," was all that Sadipe would say.

"I shall be leaving now, chief," he said. "Tomorrow I read palms; good day."

"Good day, Mr. Okukenu."

The following day about 11 o'clock Sadipe, who had donned his African costume, took up his grain bag of curios and wended his way to the house where he had made a reputation as a seer. He found the maids in cheerful mood and glad to see him. They invited him into the servants' sitting room, which had been tidied up, and he took an arm-chair and began to explain to them why he had called again, so early after his last visit. He said he was thinking of returning to his own country in a very few days, as the climate of England was much too severe to one who had always lived in a tropical country, and as the winter was coming on and as it promised to be a severe one, he would very probably go to Liverpool in the next few days and take ship for his beloved West Coast. He had called to make good his promises to the ladies to read their palms and to dispose of as many more of his African curios as they might wish to purchase of him. The young women said they were very sorry to learn that he was leaving England and they hoped he might return soon.

"I shall be very likely to return," he said; "I like your country very much, and I have met some very excellent people here. England is a great country and English people, when you know them well, are very kind and sympathetic."

Having thus prepared the way and disarmed them of suspicion as to the real object of his call, he said he was ready, if they were, to tell them their fortunes. The cook wanted hers told first, so the house girl went to the kitchen, closing the sitting-room door after her.

"I will make no charge to you for this reading. You have been kind enough to buy my trinkets and I appreciate it very much."

"Oh, thank you," said the cook, blushing; "that is very nice of you, indeed."

"Do you wish me to read the cards or your palm?" asked Sadipe.

"I think I will have you read the cards," she answered.

"Have you cards here?" asked Sadipe.

"Yes," she replied; "in that table drawer there is a new package."

"Good!" said Sadipe, opening the drawer at her direction. He took out the cards and, removing them from the case, began to shuffle them like a veteran soothsayer. The girl drew her chair up to the table and Sadipe passed the cards to her and asked her to cut them in three equal parts. With a great deal of seriousness the girl complied with his request. Sadipe picked up the first part of the three sections, ran them over once or twice before saying a word to her, shook his head, smiled meaningly, and said:

"My young lady, it is better to be born lucky than rich." Laying down a card on the table—the ace of diamonds—he continued: "there is on its way to you a letter from a distant land which contains the best news you have ever received. Following this letter will come to you a sum of money, which you have been expecting for years but feared you would never get, and you will be rich the remainder of your days."

The girl gasped and attempted to speak.

"Wait a moment," he said; "there is some sad news here for you," laying down the ten of spades, "but it is not serious. A relative whom you have never met—an old man who was very rich—is dead. He was some relation to your mother. I see a woman here," he said, showing her the queen of hearts, "who"—

The girl could wait no longer and burst out with the information that the dead man pictured in the cards was her uncle Algernon who had gone out to Australia before she was born, to engage in sheep raising. Then she wept a little, but soon recovered her composure. Sadipe took up the next section.

"You have had a proposal of marriage within the past nine days from a man who knows what I have just told you. He is a messenger in the office of the lawyers from where you will get the letter telling you of your good fortune. If you are wise you will have nothing to do with this man, who is merely a fortune hunter and doesn't love you."

"Oh!" she said, "that is Martin Coverdale."

The king of spades happened to be the next card Sadipe picked up, so he took a chance and guessed what sort of chap Martin looked like. "He is a tall, dark featured man, with very black hair, and dresses well."

"That's Martin," said the girl, and with that Sadipe threw down the king of spades, where she could see it. The girl gazed at it intently for a moment and said, "I'll never marry him."

Taking up the last section, Sadipe said: "Good hearts follow you," throwing down the ten of hearts, "the man who loves you most is the one you think of least, but he is an honest, true-hearted man, and if you marry him will make you a good husband. He is neither poor nor rich, but he has enough to make you comfortable. You met him in a gathering not long ago and shunned him. See," he said, "there's the room" (throwing down the four of clubs) "and there are the people" (throwing down the ten of clubs). The girl was dumfounded, and began to confirm Sadipe's guess.

"That man is Barney Huddleston," she said, "and as true as you live we met at a party the other night, and I avoided him. And you say he loves me?"

"As surely as you live, miss, and better than any man you know. He worships you."

The girl's face beamed with smiles. Sadipe shuffled the cards twice more and told her the same story each time and she was *happy* ever afterwards.

Then she bought a great quantity of his trinkets and gave him 25 shillings as a present for the good news he had brought her.

NOTES TO THE TEXT

1. During his long career as a newspaper reporter and editor, John Edward Bruce often wrote under pen names, including Rising Sun and, beginning in 1884, Bruce-Grit (or Bruce Grit), a byline attesting to his journalistic indomitability, which was apparently given to him by Thomas Fortune, editor of the *New York Age*.

2. The powerful Yoruba kingdom of Oyo dominated both Benin and Dahomey until the start of the eighteenth century, when its power diminished and the Yoruba people were divided among several smaller states. Today the approximately fifteen million Yorubas live mainly in southwest Nigeria.

3. A region in northern Nigeria and at one time a major Yoruba kingdom.

4. As the rest of the serial will reveal, it is not clear exactly when or even how this could occur. Perhaps Sadipe Okukenu, the black sleuth, graduates from Eton (which is a prep school rather than an institution of higher learning) during the three years that readers are told have elapsed at the start of chapter 11; however, the serial strongly suggests that he starts working for the International Detective Agency immediately after his disappointing experience at Eckington College in the American South.

5. A Roman copy of a fourth-century B.C. Greek bronze statue, the Apollo Belvedere was considered to be the greatest classical sculpture by neoclassicists. Found in Nero's villa in what is now Anzio, the marble statue is on display at the Vatican Museum.

6. The 1808 date, probably included for the edification of Bruce's readers, is problematic because other information in the serial suggests that the theft of the diamond takes place after 1900, which would make De Forrest

(presumably the "son" referred to here) at least ninety-two and not sixty-eight, as the next paragraph but one suggests.

7. Founded in 1600, the British East India Company gradually came to control much of the subcontinent. The British government began to supervise and reform the company in 1773, put an end to its monopoly in 1813, reduced it to a wholly administrative agency in 1833, and finally disbanded it in the wake of the 1857–58 Indian mutiny. See Peter J. King, "East India Company, British," *Grolier Multimedia Encyclopedia*, 1993 ed.

8. Born in Great Britain in 1853, Cecil John Rhodes arrived in southern Africa in 1870. When diamonds were discovered in Kimberley in 1871, Rhodes journeyed there, founded De Beers Consolidated Mines, and came to control nine-tenths of the world's diamond output. The renowned Open Mine produced more than 14,500,000 carats of diamonds between 1871 and 1914. See L. H. Gann, "Rhodes, Cecil John," *Grolier Multimedia Encyclopedia*, 1993 ed., and Alan C. G. Best, "Kimberley," ibid. Far inland from the Atlantic and Indian Oceans, Kimberley serves as a key rail junction, but it does not have a waterfront.

9. In 1806, the British annexed the quarter-of-a-million-square-mile territory around the Cape of Good Hope, which was originally settled by the Dutch, and named it Cape Colony; with the establishment of the Union of South Africa in 1910 it became Cape Province.

10. The reference is to Moses da Rocha of Lagos, one of many Africans with whom Bruce corresponded.

11. Significantly, but for the omission of Portuguese, these are the languages spoken in the nations which were or aspired to be colonial powers in Africa.

12. Presumably Bruce based this character on the similarly named Majola Agbebi, the Yoruba Baptist leader to whom he was introduced by Edward Blyden during Agbebi's visit to the United States in 1903. In an essay entitled "Notes on Negro American Influences on the Emergence of African Nationalism" (*Journal of African History* 1 [1960]: 299–312), George Shepperson reports that Agbebi's ideas caused Bruce to embrace and cherish fully his own blackness, and that in 1907 (the year *The Black Sleuth* began appearing in *McGirt's Magazine*) Bruce led a group of black New Yorkers who "sought to get 11 October observed each year as 'Majola Agbebi Day'" (309–

10). Agbebi was also an honorary member of the Negro Society for Historical Research, which Bruce co-founded in 1911.

13. The assertion that Sadipe is in America at the time that Mojola and De Forrest meet and the latter purchases the diamond from the former is problematic, unless Mojola is unaware that his brother has been working as a detective in Europe for many months.

14. This reversal of pervasive binary oppositions such as black versus white, light versus dark, and good versus evil—oppositions that bolstered anti–African and anti–African American propaganda—was notable for Bruce's day and no doubt had a profound effect on his black readers.

15. The amazement that Mojola recalls experiencing here resembles that expressed by the young Olaudah Equiano in chapter 4 of his *Narrative* (1789; reprinted as *Equiano's Travels*, ed. Paul Edwards [London: Heinemann, 1967]) in response to the mechanical inventions of whites: "I thought that these people were all made up of wonders" (34).

16. It is unclear from Bruce's handwritten correction whether he wanted the words "than reality" to appear after "hypocrisy" or "heathen."

17. Bruce's reference to "hollowness" here anticipates T. S. Eliot's "The Hollow Men" (1925). Eliot uses a quotation from Joseph Conrad's *Heart of Darkness* (1899)—"Mistah Kurtz—he dead"—as the epigraph to this poem, implying that the civilization and missionary impulse of Europeans like Conrad's Kurtz are actually hollow. Moreover, Mojola's juxtaposition of London and Africa recalls *Heart of Darkness,* but he rejects that novel's ambiguity, particularly in statements such as, "In the course of a few months I was able to [make my way back home], and I do not now regret that I left the 'centre of civilization' and returned to the land of 'darkness and barbarism,' as Africa is ignorantly styled by those who do not know better, and who are accustomed . . . to reason with their prejudices."

18. This assertion of the African origin of modern civilization closely resembles those to be found in Bruce's essays, such as "The Importance of Thinking Black" (1917), in Peter Gilbert, ed., *The Selected Writings of John Edward Bruce: Militant Black Journalist* (New York: Arno, 1971), 131–33: "Whatever of theology, of laws, of civil government, of art, philosophy or science the governing races, who are today in a death grapple in Europe, know had their beginnings in Africa. The Greeks and Romans got them from these

blacks, Modern Europe from the Greeks and Romans. These they have improved upon and made their own, entirely forgetting their debt to the grey-haired mother of civilization—Africa" (132).

19. In Acts 10:34–35, Peter states, "Now I really understand that God is no respecter of persons, but in every nation he who fears him and does what is right is acceptable to him."

20. Notably, Bruce here attributes prejudice against Africans to specific forms of discourse, i.e., the writings of white missionaries and journalists.

21. In contrast to later declarations that the diamond is from South Africa, Mojola here seems to suggest that the gem comes from Yorubaland, which is rather odd, given the fact that this meeting takes place in Kimberley.

22. Although the words *"To be continued"* do not appear at the end of chapter 3, this has to be the end of the second installment of the serial because the pages from *McGirt's Magazine* for chapter 3 in the Bruce Papers are 24 and 25 while those for chapter 4 are 8, 9, and 10, clearly indicating different issues of the periodical.

23. See Hamlet's speech to Horatio: "Our indiscretion sometimes serves us well, / When our deep plots do pall: and that should learn us / There's a divinity that shapes our ends, / Rough-hew them how we will" (*Hamlet* 5.2.8–11).

24. Rhodes died 26 March 1902, at the age of forty-eight.

25. Although Bruce's handwritten correction is ambiguous here, it appears that he intended to replace the words "seeing the realization of," which were printed in *McGirt's*, with "realizing."

26. Mojola here echoes Bruce's argument in his essay "The Stronger Nations vs. the Weaker Nations" (*Voice of the Negro* 2 [April 1905]: 256–57): "The evident design and purpose of the Almighty in 'fixing the bounds and habitations of nations' manifestly was that nations should develop and grow under their own 'vine and fig tree' without molestation, else why the command 'Thou shalt not covet they neighbor's house, his ox, nor his ass, nor anything that is his.' The language is mandatory, it says 'Thou shalt not.' This being true, why are . . . the strong nations under the pretext of civilizing and Christianizing people, who are peacefully pursuing their own course[,] . . . establishing 'spheres of influence,' annexing territory, and forcing their civilization and religion upon them?" (257).

27. The phrase "Africa for the Africans" is most often (and accurately)

associated with the Garvey movement. However, the phrase was used by Martin Delany in the mid-nineteenth century and perhaps can be traced even further back.

28. In the text a word between "and" and "has," which apparently has four letters, is indecipherable. Perhaps it is "even" or "ever." The sentence remains problematic, however, because it suggests the "African" has "obligingly died" when clearly Mojola is referring to the death of the "white man."

29. In 49 B.C., Julius Caesar and his troops crossed the Rubicon river, the boundary between Gaul and Italy, in violation of an order by the Roman Senate. Caesar's irrevocable step ensured that a civil war would ensue.

30. At the 1884–85 Berlin Conference, European powers met to partition Africa, formalizing and accelerating the so-called scramble for the continent.

31. This passage, like several others in the serial, is pervaded by Ethiopianism, the teleological and primarily African American view of history inspired by Psalms 68:31: "Princes shall come out of Egypt, Ethiopia shall soon stretch forth her hands unto God." Ethiopia here, as elsewhere in the Bible, refers not to the East African nation also known as Abyssinia but rather to all of Africa south of Egypt and thus the continent generally. Dating back to the late 1700s, Ethiopianism, with its prediction of a glorious future for people of African descent, can be found in sermons, pamphlets, speeches, and articles by black Americans throughout the nineteenth century as well as African American literary works about Africa in the first half of the twentieth century. For more information on Ethiopianism, see St. Clair Drake, *The Redemption of Africa and Black Religion* (Chicago: Third World, 1970); Wilson J. Moses, *The Golden Age of Black Nationalism, 1850–1925* (1978; reprint, New York: Oxford University Press, 1988), and *The Wings of Ethiopia: Studies in African-American Life and Letters* (Ames: Iowa State University Press, 1990); Eric J. Sundquist, *To Wake the Nations: Race in the Making of American Literature* (Cambridge: Harvard University Press, 1993), 551–63; and Gruesser, *Black on Black: Twentieth-Century African American Literature about Africa* (Lexington: University Press of Kentucky, 2000), 1–14.

32. Mojola here combines lines from different stanzas of Burns's 1795 poem. The last two lines of the first stanza are "The rank is but the guinea stamp; / The Man's the gowd [gold] for a' that!" Lines four and five of the sec-

ond stanza are similar but not identical to the second line Mojola quotes: "A Man's a Man for a' that! / For a' that an' a' that."

33. The Southern mariner's doubts about the abilities of a "nigger" detective expressed in the first chapter contradict his assertion of conversion here; however, Bruce's purpose in *The Black Sleuth* is not to convert prejudiced whites like De Forrest but rather his black readers who may accept white racist rhetoric about African Americans and Africans.

34. Perhaps Captain De Forrest has in mind the verse that concludes Christ's parable of the laborers: "Even so the last shall be first, and the first last: for many be called, but few are chosen" (Matt. 20:16).

35. In classical mythology, the deity of dreams and, by extension, sleep.

36. Bruce is quoting from the last two lines of stanza twelve of "To the Lady Margaret, Countess of Cumberland" by the English lyricist and playwright Samuel Daniel (1562–1619):

> Knowing the heart of man is set to be
> The center of this world, about the which
> These revolutions of disturbances
> Still roll, where all th' aspects of misery
> Predominate, whose strong effects are such
> As he must bear, being powerless to redress,
> And that unless above himself he can
> Erect himself, how poor a thing is man!

37. This number is problematic. We are told that Sadipe is three years younger than his brother Mojola, yet Mojola is described as being only nineteen or twenty when he meets De Forrest, an event that occurs no earlier than 1902, the year Cecil Rhodes died. Moreover, if Mojola's trip to England (and Sadipe's to America) takes places three or more years earlier, as other evidence in the serial suggests, then the older Okukenu brother is at most seventeen when he travels to England and his brother a mere fourteen when he crosses the Atlantic with Barnard.

38. The German romantic novelist Jean Paul Richter (1763–1825), who wrote under the pseudonym Jean Paul.

39. Here and elsewhere Sadipe's bright future is described in terms similar to those used by his brother Mojola (and later himself) to describe Africa. This suggests that the younger Okukenu, the black sleuth, can be read as an allegorical figure representing the continent or the black world generally.

40. Later, however, we are told that Mrs. Pelham had been a teacher "in a boys' academy near Boston."

41. Related to the Ashantis, the Fanti people live along the southern coast of Ghana.

42. The forty-four-foot-high, white marble Peace Monument was erected in 1877–78 to memorialize those who died at sea during the Civil War. The statue consists of several figures, including History, Grief, Victory, and Peace, and bears the inscription "In memory of the officers, seamen, and marines of the United States who fell in defense of the Union and liberty of their country, 1861–1865." See *The Peace Monument*, 1 November 1999, Architect of the Capitol, Office of the Curator, 17 July 2000, http://www.aoc.gov/art/peace_monument.htm.

43. Like Harriet A. Jacobs in chapter 12 of *Incidents in the Life of a Slave Girl* (1861; reprint, Jean Fagan Yellin, ed. [Cambridge: Harvard University Press, 1987]), here and elsewhere Bruce reverses the standard use of dialect in American writing by having certain white characters speak in a pronounced dialect while his black protagonist and other black characters use impeccable English.

44. The words *"To be continued"* do not appear at the end of this chapter; nevertheless, this is the end of the fifth installment of the serial.

45. The first eleven paragraphs of chapter 7 are a rehash, often verbatim, of the last seven paragraphs of chapter 6, and thus are not printed in the main text. The beginning of chapter 7 as it appears in the Bruce Papers can be found in Appendix A. Handwritten notes at the start of chapter 7 in the Bruce Papers read "Duplicate chapter," "Rewrite," and "Don't destroy." Some of the significant changes and additions in this alternative version are that the train for Eckington leaves at 12:37, the insolent ticket-taker is suspended for two days without pay for his treatment of Sadipe, and the younger Okukenu brother experiences his second shock at 1:25.

46. Bruce's portrayal of "shiftless, aimless white loafers" here recalls the depiction of the "mighty ornery lot" of poor white "loafers" in a "one-horse town" that is "pretty well down the State of Arkansaw" in chapter 21 of Mark Twain's *Adventures of Huckleberry Finn* (1885; reprint, Thomas Cooley, ed., 3d ed. [New York: Norton, 1999], 154, 153).

47. This is the eleventh and final stanza of Henry Wadsworth Longfellow's "The Day Is Done."

48. As I discuss in the Introduction, Bruce appears to be quite intentionally ridiculing Booker T. Washington and his Tuskegee Institute in this chapter and the two chapters that follow.

49. Popular in England from 1865 to 1885 and the United States from 1875 to 1890, the Queen Anne revival imitated the eighteenth-century, English architectural style named for the monarch who ruled from 1702 to 1714.

50. The final two sentences of this paragraph would read more clearly if the period after "fun" were removed and the comma after "him" were changed to a semicolon.

51. The Irish composer Michael William Balfe (1808–70) wrote the music for the light opera *The Bohemian Girl* (1843).

52. Richard Wagner's opera *Tannhäuser* was completed and first performed in 1845.

53. The authors referred to are the African American poet Paul Laurence Dunbar (1872–1906) and James Ephraim McGirt (1874–1930), editor of *McGirt's Magazine* (in which *The Black Sleuth* was published), whose poetry and prose often appeared in the journal.

54. "Rocked in the Cradle of the Deep," by the American poet Emma Willard (1787–1870), was set to music by the English-born composer Joseph P. Knight (1812–87).

55. Francesco Paulo Tosti (1846–1916) wrote many popular songs in both Italian and English, including "Good-bye," "At Vespers," and "Amore."

56. Henry Flagler built the Ponce de Leon Hotel in St. Augustine, Florida; it was completed in 1885.

57. In Hebrews 7:3, Paul describes Melchisedech, the king of Salem who blessed Abraham, as follows: "Without father, without mother, without genealogy, having neither beginning of days nor end of life, but likened to the Son of God, he continues a priest forever."

58. Written at the bottom of the final page of this installment of the serial in the Bruce Papers are the words "Missing Chapter"; however, what this refers to is unknown.

59. Methodist Episcopal.

60. In Homer, the Cimmerians are far western or northern people said to live in perpetual darkness.

61. Through the name of this missionary Bruce may be slyly alluding to

the Skinner Expedition to Abyssinia, a target of one of his most staunchly anti-colonial and anti-imperial essays, "The Dusky Kings of Africa and the Islands of the Sea" (*Voice of the Negro* 2 [August 1905]: 573–75). As he did previously in Mojola's interview with De Forrest, in this episode involving the Rev. Skinner, Bruce provides an early condemnation of missionary activity on the continent, a position that would be echoed in the texts about Africa by later black American writers, particularly Langston Hughes, Richard Wright, Lorraine Hansberry, and Alice Walker.

62. The English clergyman Reginald Heber (1783–1826) became bishop of Calcutta in 1823. Although several volumes of his poetry and sermons were published, he is most famous as the writer of the words to such well-known hymns as "From Greenland's Icy Mountains" (1819; set to music by Lowell Mason in 1823) and "Trinity Sunday" ("Holy, Holy, Holy"). The lyrics of the former, to which Sadipe objects so strenuously, can be found in *Hymns of the Centuries*, ed. Benjamin Shepard (New York: Barnes, 1911), 333, and are as follows:

> From Greenland's icy mountains,
> From India's coral strand,
> Where Afric's sunny fountains
> Roll down their golden sand,
> From many an ancient river,
> From many a palmy plain,
> They call us to deliver
> Their land from error's chain.
>
> What though the spicy breezes
> Blow soft o'er Ceylon's isle;
> Though ev'ry prospect pleases,
> And only man is vile:
> In vain with lavish kindness
> The gifts of God are strown;
> The heathen in his blindness
> Bows down to wood and stone.
>
> Can we, whose souls are lighted
> With wisdom from on high,
> Can we to men benighted

The lamp of life deny?
Salvation! O salvation!
The joyful sound proclaim,
Till each remotest nation
Has learned Messiah's name.

Waft, waft, ye winds, His story,
And you, ye waters, roll,
Till like a sea of glory
It spreads from pole to pole;
Till o'er our ransomed nature
The Lamb for sinners slain,
Redeemer, King, Creator,
In bliss returns to reign. Amen.

63. The text reads "Assistant Principal Swift" here, but this is clearly an error.

64. The phrase "those who sit in darkness" may originally derive from Matthew 4:16—"The people who sat in darkness have seen a great light, and upon those who sat in the region and shadow of death, a light has arisen." Today, however, it is most often associated with Mark Twain's anti-imperialist essay, "To the Person Sitting in Darkness" (1901).

65. Sadipe's argument here closely resembles one made in some of the oratories of the Seneca chief Sa-Go-Ye-Wat-Ha (1758–1830), also known as Red Jacket. Early in his career as a journalist, Bruce wrote for the Cherokee nation's newspaper, the *Cherokee Advocate*.

66. A water-cooled machine gun with a single barrel named after its American-born English inventor, Sir Hiram S. Maxim (1840–1916).

67. Sadipe's thesis here echoes that of Bruce's article "The Stronger Nations vs. the Weaker Nations."

68. The significance of the preceding scene, one of the most memorable in the novel, is addressed at some length in the Introduction.

69. Between the headline and the story proper, there are two short summaries that introduce the article.

70. A headline in extremely large type.

71. Although the serial reads "forenoon" here, such a meeting could have taken place only in the afternoon.

72. Polonius offers this advice to Laertes in *Hamlet* 1.3.75.

73. Beginning with this installment, the remainder of the serial lacks printed chapter numbers; however, handwritten notes in the margins identify the numbers of most of these chapters.

74. Earlier Mr. Hunter's organization was referred to as the International Detective Agency or Bureau.

75. The chronology of events is problematic here. Sadipe has been working for Hunter's agency for at least three years before De Forrest obtains the diamond that is later stolen. The date of Sadipe's letter to De Mortie indicates it was written before 1900; meanwhile, given Mojola's reference to the death of Cecil Rhodes in his conversation with De Forrest, the captain could not have purchased the gem before 1902.

76. This seems to contradict Bruce's earlier description of De Forrest as someone with an "experienced eye" for diamonds, though perhaps the captain is feigning ignorance here.

77. Yielding or containing gold; presumably used metaphorically here by Bruce.

78. Knight Commander of the Bath, Regular Army.

79. In the mid-sixth century B.C., the last king of Lydia, renowned for his great wealth.

80. This quotation comes from chapter 18 of *The Prince* (1513) by Niccolò Machiavelli (1469–1527).

81. There are intriguing connections between Bruce's fictional Bradshawe and a notorious thief named Adam Worth (1844–1901), described by the Pinkerton detective agency as "the most remarkable, most successful and most dangerous professional criminal known in modern times" (quoted in Ben MacIntyre, "The Disappearing Duchess," *New York Times Magazine*, 31 July 1994: 30). The model for Arthur Conan Doyle's Professor Moriarty, Worth was born in the United States, settled in London, and coordinated a crime syndicate stretching from Europe to Asia Minor to South Africa. For more on Worth, see MacIntyre, *The Napoleon of Crime: The Life and Times of Adam Worth, Master Thief* (New York: Farrar, Straus and Giroux, 1997), and James D. Horan, *The Pinkertons: The Detective Dynasty That Made History* (New York: Crown, 1967), 280–320.

82. Earlier it was the "Norman K. Peters."

83. One or more lines are missing in the serial here, which reads, ". . . the attention of the habitues [line break] ough hat, which set off. . . ."

84. Electroliers are chandeliers for electric lamps.

85. Because the diamond has not yet been stolen, this statement is problematic, as is the time sequence in this paragraph and in this chapter as a whole.

86. Here the serial shifts from Sadipe's first person report of what transpired in Mr. Stoughton's rooms to the third person, even though quotation marks continue to be used until the last six paragraphs of the chapter. Moreover, in those concluding paragraphs, Sadipe is described as going to see Mr. Hunter immediately following his encounter with the suspicious colonel; however, the chapter begins with Sadipe already engaged in a conversation with his employer.

87. As other passages indicate, Bruce clearly desires to present Bradshawe as a criminal mastermind. Here, however, the "colonel" proves to be a rather clumsy con man, forgetting what he said a few moments earlier about his relationship to Miss Crenshawe and failing to use an alias when referring to her.

88. A cracksman is a burglar or housebreaker.

89. The three kingdoms presumably are England, Scotland, and Ireland.

90. In Greek myth, Argus was a giant with a hundred eyes.

91. By locating the initial encounter between Hunter and Bradshawe in Vienna, Bruce may be acknowledging his debt to the creator of detective fiction, Edgar Allan Poe. In "The Purloined Letter" (1844; reprint, in *The Complete Tales and Poems of Edgar Allan Poe* [New York: Modern Library, 1938], 208–22), Poe's detective, C. Auguste Dupin, explains that he has a personal motive for ensuring that the Minister D——— knows who has outwitted him, namely that his adversary once did Dupin an "evil turn" in Vienna for which Dupin warned D——— he would repay him (222).

92. This is the only concrete date in the serial, although the "18—" on Sadipe's letter to General De Mortie and Mojola's reference to Cecil Rhodes's death in his conversation with De Forrest suggest that Sadipe's sojourn in America occurs at the end of the nineteenth century and the plot to steal De Forrest's diamond takes place early in the twentieth.

93. Another allusion to *Hamlet;* however, this specific line does not appear in the tragedy.

94. Bruce's knowledge of instrumental and choral music, apparent in this paragraph and elsewhere in the serial, is not surprising given that one of his two wives was an opera singer and he himself wrote not only the lyrics but the music to songs. See Gilbert, *Selected Writings of Bruce*, 1.

95. This is the first mention of Bradshawe's eyepiece.

96. On the contrary, this is the first reference to such a dinner. All that has been mentioned so far is the lunch at which Miss Crenshawe attracts De Forrest's attention. Later in this chapter, a dinner at which Bradshawe introduces De Forrest to Crenshawe will be described.

97. The phrase "there's a sucker born every minute" is attributed to the American showman P. T. Barnum (1810–91).

98. This statement and Hunter's note in the previous paragraph are problematic because Sadipe already knows where Bradshawe and the others live, having followed the "colonel" home after spotting him at the music hall.

99. In chiromancy, the mount of Venus refers to the fleshy part of the hand below the thumb.

100. Oddly, Sadipe stops speaking in pidgin English here and does not speak it again.

101. Readers who wish to read the serial the way it appears in the Bruce Papers on microfilm should proceed directly to Appendix B. However, the evidence that the final two installments somehow became inverted is so compelling that they have been reversed here. See the Editor's Note in the Introduction for a thorough explanation.

102. How Sadipe and Hunter come to know this is unclear. Perhaps this is something the maid told the disguised detective that was not reported in the previous chapter; however, when he himself mentions this piece of information to her in the final installment, his phrasing suggests that she was not the source of this information.

103. The reference to this person as the "cook" here is very likely a mistake. Up until this point, the servants in the house that Sadipe has dealt with have been consistently referred to as "maids"—four times in the previous two chapters and once in this installment.

104. In contrast to all the other installments, in this section quotations from Sadipe and the maid are consistently printed within the same paragraph rather than presented in different paragraphs. Perhaps this was done to save space, as this installment comprises so much dialogue, most of it brief. For

consistency's sake, the paragraphs of this section have been broken up here and in Appendix B.

105. This hardly seems possible, as Sadipe waited on the "quartet" at lunch only three days before this.

106. Although this sequence reads better than the one in the Bruce Papers on microfilm (and Appendix B), in neither version is the novel satisfactorily resolved. The words "(*To be continued.*)" at the end of the final installment clearly indicate that Bruce did not intend for this to be the conclusion of the serial. Oddly, there was not an installment of *The Black Sleuth* in the next and final issue of *McGirt's Magazine,* October/November/ December 1909. For the editor's conjecture as to what happens following the events described in chapter 17, see the Introduction.